WASH BASIN STREET BLUES

Mark O'Sullivan

WOLFHOUND PRESS

First published 1995 by
WOLFHOUND PRESS Ltd
68 Mountjoy Square
Dublin 1

This book is fiction. All characters, incidents and names have no connection with any persons living or dead. Any apparent resemblance is purely coincidental.

Wolfhound Press receives financial assistance from the Arts Council/An Chomhairle Ealaíon, Dublin.

British Library Cataloguing in Publication Data
A catalogue record for this book is available from the British Library.

ISBN 0-86327-467-6

The poem in Chapter 22 is 'Life and Nature' by Archibald Lampman (1861-99)

Cover illustration: Katharine White
Cover design: Joe Gervin
Typesetting: Wolfhound Press
Printed by the Guernsey Press Co Ltd, Guernsey, Channel Isles

CHAPTER 1

'Don't move,' the muffled voice warned, 'and don't close your eyes or we'll be here all day.'

Molly and Peter Delaney sat stiffly side by side on a low couch in the photographer's musty studio. Behind them, their niece Nora Canavan stood. Her left hand rested on Peter's shoulder, her right on Molly's. A faded backdrop showed a cobbled path between tall trees with pale statues of Roman gods and goddesses peeping from the shadows. All three, like statues themselves now, waited as old Mr O'Neill fumbled about under the threadbare cloth hanging down behind the big box camera.

The notion of a 'family portrait' both pleased Nora and left her feeling wistful. On the one hand it was a declaration to the world that they were indeed a family, she and her aunt and uncle, and that was good. However, she'd only had her photograph taken once before. That was nine years ago when her world was very different. A sulky seven-year-old she was then, surrounded by her mother and father and the lively two-year-old twins, Denis and Ritchie.

Her mother's calm smile had shown no evidence of the illness that, in a few short years, would take her so cruelly from them. Her father's contented young face revealed nothing of the terrible depths to which alcohol would drag him. Nor did it even vaguely hint at his final emergence from those depths to a life spent alone in the railwayman's cottage in Inchicore, once the Canavan family home.

The grinning boys had no inkling then that they would be sent from Dublin to live in New York. And Nora, in spite of her glum features on that day, could not have imagined that she would find herself living in Tipperary with an aunt and uncle she had never met until the day of her mother's funeral.

'The divil fire it,' Mr O'Neill rasped as he raised himself from his crouched position and shook off the cloth covering his wizened old head. 'I forgot to put in the plate.'

He waddled away to the door, sneezing and blowing into a large and not very clean handkerchief.

'Nothing worse than a summer cold,' Peter called after him.

'If I could light a fire itself,' the old man complained, 'sbut the price of coal these days, I might as well be burning pound notes. Pure desperate it is.'

Two years had passed since that bitter morning in Glasnevin cemetery. Nora's reluctant arrival in this town and the unexpected events that followed were, in many ways, just a distant memory now. There were moments of loneliness and regret for all she had lost but, as time passed, she realised, too, how much she had gained.

Her life in Tipperary was comfortable in comparison to her previous existence. Her aunt and uncle had a shop and ran the only cinema in town. Having no children of their own they were completely devoted to her.

She had friends too, classmates in the convent school. There was Áine, with her carroty hair and a smiling face that was a vast sea of freckles. Siobhán was quiet and bookish and sometimes a little too serious for Áine and Nora's liking. Yet it was she who always seemed to notice first when that misty look of longing appeared in Nora's eyes; she who always found some distraction to lift her spirits.

And then there was her father. Strange as it often seemed, Nora had never been closer to him than she was now. They met, at most, just twice a month. From time to time, she doubted whether he had done the right thing by agreeing to split up his family. With each visit, these doubts crumbled a little more.

From the beginning he had made his only real choice quite clear. He could not work the long hours in the railway and take proper care of his children. The obvious alternative was for Nora to take her mother's place in the home. This he would not allow her to do. She had a special talent and he wanted her to have every chance to make the most of it.

'And the coal these times, you'd get more heat out of a stone. Sure, it's pure desperate,' Peter observed. (Mr O'Neill looked at him suspiciously over his pince-nez glasses. On their way to his studio, Peter had told them of the old man's favourite phrase — 'pure desperate'. So far they'd heard it at least five times.)

'It is,' the photographer muttered, 'Pure...downright disgraceful.'

Molly turned to hide her wide grin but Nora wasn't amused. She longed to escape from the dust-laden room and the pangs of jealous guilt that bothered her.

From the moment she'd heard of Peter's upcoming trip to America she had felt this unpleasant mixture of emotions. It wasn't that she begrudged him his opportunity. She'd seen how hard he'd worked to organise the trip by a group of hurlers from the county. His enthusiasm knew no bounds, so determined was he to break down the Civil War differences that blighted Tipperary — and all of Ireland for that matter. Men who only a short while before were trying to kill each other, were now to travel as a team, and Peter would join them as an official.

Nora, however, could only think of her brothers so far

away and the unliklihood of meeting them for a very long time yet. Their frequent letters reassured her that they'd settled in well with Phil, her father's brother, and his American wife, Fay. She had no reason to doubt that in America they had a better life than they could have dreamed of back in Inchicore. Still, the excitement surrounding Peter's trip left her secretly miserable.

Unfortunately for Nora, Peter's enthusiasm hadn't stopped at his planning of the hurling trip. When the idea occurred to him a few weeks previously of 'killing two birds with the one stone', as he'd put it, his mind wasn't to be changed. He had to have a photograph taken for his passport, so why not have the 'family portrait' done also, he'd declared.

'Wouldn't it be grand,' he'd added, 'to send one to the boys in New York and to Alec in Paris.'

If Dublin was the place of Nora's past and Tipperary that of her present, then Paris was where her future lay. Alec Smithson was the guiding light to that future.

During her first months in town Alec, the piano man at Peter's cinema, had become her inspiration. A ravaged survivor of the Great War, he'd played with impossible elegance in spite of a missing finger and scarred hands. He had finally gone to Paris to fulfil his musical destiny leaving Nora to take his place at the battered, but nonetheless tuneful piano. For music was the gift her father was so anxious that she develop and, by now, it had become the precious thread holding her whole being together.

She was never happier or more fully alive than when she sat down before the keys of the piano. Even in the rowdy atmosphere of the Stella cinema where she played every weekend, her concentration was so intense that she heard nothing but the measured tones of the instrument.

On her visits to Dublin, her father would take her to Mrs Teehan's house on the South Circular Road. Here, in the more sedate setting of her teacher's parlour she would hone her skills. Mrs Teehan had every confidence that Nora would win the Waldsworth Scholarship next year, go to the Paris Conservatoire of Music and move on to a career as a pianist.

Mr O'Neill blustered back into the studio, tut-tutting to himself in agitation.

'There's nothing I hate worse than wasting time,' he said.

'Time is money,' Peter agreed.

'If only it was,' the old man wheezed, 'I'd be a rich man at my age.'

Nora withdrew her hand from Molly's shoulder and fidgeted with the ridiculously large white moth of ribbon in her strawy hair.

'Is she at the bow again, Peter?' Molly asked of her husband.

'Not at all,' he chuckled, 'she's only picking her nose.'

'I am not,' Nora protested. 'Anyway, I'm too old for this stupid thing. I'm nearly sixteen.'

Molly had prepared the ribbon and had refused to listen to Nora's complaints about it. In fact, Nora had been tempted to tell her aunt that if she could see properly she'd realise how silly the thing looked. She was glad she hadn't. Molly's quickly failing eyesight was too serious a matter.

Her aunt had already lost the sight in her left eye and there was little hope for the other one. Her dependence on Peter and Nora was growing by the day, though she never complained or showed any sign of frustration. Nora had, at first, thought that Molly was giving in too easily and preparing herself too readily for the mysterious universe of the blind. Once she had even found her in the kitchen with her eyes shut tight, feeling her way around the pots and pans and the crockery on the dresser.

'I'm trying to remember with my hands,' Molly had explained, laughing at the strangeness of her own words.

Soon, however, Nora realised that her aunt was a practical woman, as practical in this matter as in any other. If blindness should come, Molly would not allow it to change her life. In the darkness of the photographic studio, Nora pressed gently on Molly's shoulder as if to return to her some of that strength of will she had received in her own time of crisis.

'Not a budge now.' Mr O'Neill was under his tattered cloth again.

'What in the name of God did he want a plate for anyway?' Molly whispered.

'A photographic plate, Molly,' Peter explained. 'It's for —'

'Cripes, Mr Delaney,' the old man yelped, 'Would you ever stop moving your mouth or we'll never finish this photograph, never mind do the next one.'

Nora's stifled laughter ended almost before it had begun.

'I don't know what you're giggling at,' Peter told her without taking his eyes from the camera. 'You're next.'

The room was lit by a momentary flash. A sharp, powdery tang filled their nostrils and Molly and Peter relaxed, breathing out a huge sigh of relief. For Nora, however, there was no such relief.

'Me?' she exclaimed, 'On my own?'

Her objections to the photograph proved as futile as those she'd raised to the white ribbon. She might even have managed a wry smile if Peter hadn't taken her by surprise again just as the second explosion of light erupted.

'You can't have a passport without a photograph,' he called from behind the camera.

If the world was too dark for Molly as they emerged from Mr O'Neill's house on to Friary Street, it was almost too bright for Nora to bear. Reflected from the windowpanes along the street, the sun made her dizzy. She seemed to be floating rather than walking, like in a dream of flight.

'What did you mean about a passport?' she asked tentatively, 'and why didn't you get your own picture taken?'

Peter's explanation came to her as if he was speaking from some high, distant platform and she was a lost child among the listening crowd.

Molly was to go down to Cork next month to meet a doctor at the eye and ear hospital there. The chances were he would be recommending an immediate operation. Since the team would be leaving for America in less than three weeks Peter would therefore have to miss the trip. Molly had tried to dissuade him but he felt he had to be with her at such a time. The other officials had agreed that Nora could travel with them. She would stay in New York with her Uncle Phil and the boys while the hurlers went on their tour of America.

Though she came up with many reasons why she shouldn't go, Nora knew deep down that she didn't want to change Peter's mind. The casualness and good humour of Peter's answers showed that he knew exactly what she was thinking.

'And what about the cinema?' she tried finally. 'Who'll sell the tickets and play the piano?'

'We won't be bothering with all that for a while,' Molly said. 'Between that picture-house and the shop, Peter hasn't time to draw breath.'

For the first time Nora was aware of how much older Peter had got since she'd come to town. The death of his brother in the Civil War and the worry over Molly's future had aged him considerably. The fact that she hadn't noticed this until now made Nora feel less than grateful for all he'd done for her and for what he now proposed to do.

'You need the rest more than I do.'

'And do you think that traipsing around America would be a rest?' Peter asked drolly. 'I'd be a stretcher case coming back out of it.'

~

On those rare occasions when there was time to think during the days that followed, Nora's mind turned constantly to Denis and Ritchie. And to New York. New York!

She'd often seen its tall buildings and crowded streets in films at the Stella Cinema and wondered if, somewhere in the passing multitudes, her brothers might have been strolling with Uncle Phil and his wife. The city, she knew, was renowned for the riches and good fortune Irish emigrants might find there.

But there were fears too, fears that crossed her mind when she thought of the boys in that huge metropolis. In its emormous network of streets and avenues, they might easily have been lost and never found. And among that vast population, greater than the whole of Ireland, there roamed gangs of criminals who lived off the weak and innocent — if she was to believe all she'd heard.

In the films, she often saw this frightful underworld of gangsters portrayed. It seemed that New York, like many other cities, had more than its fair share of these parasites, sucking the life-blood of that immense nation.

Things had been bad enough before 1920 but something happened in that year to make the situation worse. In a word it was Prohibition. When Nora first heard of Prohibition she'd thought it was a good idea. It meant that the sale of all alcoholic drink was prohibited.

However, it soon became clear that what had seemed a simple solution to an all-too-common problem brought with it many complications. When something is denied them, people will go to any lengths to get it. Alcohol was made and sold secretly and, it was said, many of those who'd never taken a drink before began to do so now. It was a kind of protest against being told how to live their lives.

The making and selling of this illegal alcohol was controlled by the gangsters. They quickly put together a vast web of criminality that threatened to engulf every man, woman and child within their reach.

Now that she was about to go there herself there were other, more immediate fears. Would Denis and Ritchie, soon eleven-years-old, have changed beyond recognition? Would they regard her as a sister any more? Had they, perhaps, in spite of their brotherly letters, never forgiven her for leaving without even saying goodbye? Would they understand that she had simply not had the heart to do so?

But her excitement outweighed her fears when on the evening before her departure, Nora took her leave of Áine and Siobhán. They didn't stay long since they knew she was busy with last-minute prepartions. As they left, Áine called out good-humouredly: 'You might get to like it out there, maybe you mightn't come back at all.'

'That's a terrible thing to say,' Siobhán cried, serious as ever.

'I was only joking,' Áine complained and was pushed towards the door by her furious friend.

'Course I'll be back,' Nora told them. They'd already gone.

She stared at the closed door for fully a minute before retreating to her room at the top of the house in Stannix Lane.

CHAPTER 2

The long winding avenue leading to the railway station was jammed with ponies and traps, charabancs and a few automobiles. Nora and Molly took all of ten minutes to weave their way through the high-spirited crowd. Somewhere behind them, Peter struggled manfully with Nora's bags. On the station platform the town's brass band did their best to tune up their instruments as gangs of children ran in and out between their ranks. It was a scene of delightful pandemonium.

Amid the confusion, Molly bombarded her niece with reminders.

'Are you sure you have the passport? And the money, where's your purse? Did we pack the new pairs of socks?'

'Molly,' Nora assured her, 'we checked everything a hundred times.'

'But you never know. We might have forgotten something. It always happens. Where's Peter? Holy God, is he lost or what?'

'He's standing behind you.'

'And about time too,' Molly said, wiping her forehead with a handkerchief.

The neat greystone station, so often a place of sad farewells in the past was transformed. It was as if everyone was celebrating a future where they and their families could travel great distances without the haunting prospect of never being able to return. The hurling party would be coming back in a very short time, having met many of the town's emigrants in cities all over America. Even those who weren't going somehow felt they would be drawn closer to their long-lost relatives.

They celebrated too because the Civil War divisions were being put aside by the men who travelled together as a team despite their differences. In his speech at the platform the parish priest, Fr Scanlon, emphasised this point. But he made many other points too. Too many. On such a grand occasion he wasn't about to change his habit of long sermons.

People began to shuffle uneasily in the respectful silence. The children, usually terrified of this large, imposing man soon began their chasing games again. Only then did the priest realise that it was time to stop talking. With a last blessing he motioned to the band to strike up a marching tune.

The team lined up and took the cheers and good wishes of the crowd before boarding the train. Nora turned quickly to Molly but couldn't speak. When she tried, Molly put a finger to her lips. Nora thought about what Molly would have to go through in the weeks to come while she herself was enjoying her adventure in New York. She didn't want to mention the operation but felt she should offer some words of encouragement.

'No need to upset yourself, Nora,' Molly said. 'Hop in there and get yourself a decent seat.'

Peter shook her hand and then quite unexpectedly, kissed her on the cheek. Again, she found she couldn't force the words past the lump in her throat.

'John Moloney will keep an eye on you for the journey,' he told her. 'He'll see you right.'

She hurried on to the train as the signalman blew his whistle for the second time. Someone guided her to a seat by the window but she was too overcome to see who it was, never mind to thank him. The train jerked forward and she caught a last glimpse of Molly and Peter as they waved and were lost in the surge of bodies along the disappearing platform. She was angry at herself for not having said goodbye properly and felt a little foolish at having been so tearful.

All around her people were talking loudly, standing up suddenly and just as suddenly sitting down, unable to contain their excitement. She felt dazed. The sun, darting in and out from behind the trees alongside the tracks, flashed before her eyes. She put her head in her hands and even though her eyelids were clamped tight, the light was still dazzling. A voice whispered in her ear through the buzz of conversation.

'Are you alright, Nora?'

Nora always felt strangely confused when she met John Moloney. He seemed too cocky, too sure of his good looks. Yet when he spoke he was so natural and good-humoured you had to reconsider your first impression. Deep down she had to admit she really liked him and she had good reason. He was a close friend of her uncle and two years back, while still a young Free State soldier, he'd saved Alec Smithson from certain death.

However, he was a Civic Guard now and often called to the house in Stannix Lane. Every time he left Nora's blood was boiling in temper. He always seemed to pick the wrong time to tease her. His favourite ruse was to tell Peter and Molly he'd seen her uptown with some young fellow. The name he'd invented for this non-existent boy was Sean-Bán. The more she protested the more he would embellish his white lie. Invariably, Nora would tell him he'd be better off catching thieves or checking the lamps on bicycles than sitting in their kitchen drinking tea and making up stories.

At this point Peter and Molly would have to intervene and amid much laughter Nora would storm out of the room, banging the door after her. When she'd calmed down she'd be left with the impression that he regarded her as a child.

This disappointed and annoyed her though she was never quite sure why his opinion of her mattered in the least. Right now, the idea of John Moloney 'keeping an eye' on her really galled her.

'Course I'm alright,' she snapped. 'The flippin' sun is blinding me.'

'I thought you might be a bit lonely after Sean-Bán.'

'Would you ever take a run and jump, I'm well able to mind myself, thank you very much.'

'What's wrong with you?' he protested with a grin. 'Did you get out on the wrong side of the bed or what?'

'No, but I got on to the wrong side of the train,' she scowled, 'beside you.'

John laughed and gave her a wide wink.

'I'll be back when you're in a better mood.'

'Don't be in any hurry.'

Now that she was left alone her mood improved. The day was filled with so much promise that her mind tuned to thoughts of the journey ahead.

In a little while they would change trains at Limerick and sometime in mid-afternoon they would reach the port of Cobh. There, for the first time in her life, she would be staying overnight in a hotel. For nine days she would sail across the Atlantic aboard the SS *Bremen*, a German ship. Then she would, at last, be meeting Denis and Ritchie and Uncle Phil and his wife, Fay. Her brothers' letters were always quite short but it was easy to see that they both liked Fay a lot. Nora was sure she would get on well with her too.

The only photograph she'd ever seen of Phil was taken just before he'd left for America. That was fifteen years ago, the year Nora was born. He was barely twenty at the time. Beneath his mop of black hair was the easy smile of someone who took things in his stride. A young man without worries, his eyes fixed firmly on the promise of a successful future.

As for Fay, Nora could conjure up only a hazy vision from the boys' words. She seemed to be generous, good-humoured and caring. In Nora's mind, Fay had become almost a sister to her own mother and Molly.

~

In the early evening of the still bright day they arrived at Cobh. They ascended the steep street from the station, not to their hotel as she'd expected but to the American Consul's Office where their passports were to be stamped.

Here, they joined the end of a long queue and by the time she had shuffled through along with the others, her legs were beginning to feel very heavy. The hurlers and officials had grown quiet by now too. When they were told their next stop was at the Steam Ship Offices they grumbled and moaned. Even John Moloney found it difficult to keep up his joking and Nora took secret delight in his discomfort.

In these offices Nora was given a slip of paper headed 'North German Lloyd Line; SS *Bremen*'. Below was listed the number of her berth. She and the rest of the hurling party would be travelling second class. John described this as the 'purgatory' between the 'heaven' of first class and the 'hell' of third class.

It was with great relief after all this that she found herself at the entrance to the States Hotel. No longer was she dreaming of luxurious bedrooms or grand dining rooms. All she wanted was a bed, any bed, to stretch her weary limbs.

But no sooner had she been shown to her room, which was small but plushly-decorated, than John came tapping on the door. A special high tea had been laid on for them, he announced, and it was to be served in five minutes. Nora stared longingly at the inviting bed.

'You can't travel on an empty stomach, girl,' John told her and she thought he was probably right.

Halfway through the meal she was dismayed to hear that a dance had been arranged for the travelling party. She began to make excuses but John insisted it would be very bad form not to stay for one dance considering all the trouble the organisers had gone to.

To her consternation she was dragged out to the floor for a set dance. She was so drained of energy she kept forgetting the moves in the Cashel Set . As soon as she'd sat down after her awkward efforts, a group gathered around her and urged her to 'give a tune' on the piano. She'd never felt so reluctant to play but there was no escape.

For two hours she accompanied a variety of singers, some quite good if you were in the mood to listen. The majority, however, were plain awful. Following their unintended changes of key was like trying to cut a path through a jungle.

In the end, it was John who put her out of her misery. He could see how worn out she looked and felt bad about keeping her up so late. To a chorus of disappointment from the others he announced that Nora was too young to be carousing at this hour. At any other time Nora would have been offended but now she let the remark pass.

She mounted the carpeted stairs of the hotel and put the singing and dancing behind her. Her arms were so leaden that she couldn't bring herself to draw the curtains. In a matter of minutes she was as deeply asleep as she'd been since she'd first heard of her trip to America.

Next morning, she was awoken early by the screeching gulls and dull thuds of loading and unloading down at the harbour below her window. For a long time she gazed sleepily at the little groups of men trudging towards the quays. In the morning stillness she could almost hear their heaves and groans as they lifted and strained.

Out in the bay, ships rose and swayed gently down on the huge, soft heartbeat of the ocean. The line of the horizon soon came into view, showing where the sea ended and the sky began. It was as if today was clearing an inviting passage to tomorrow. Only when John knocked at the door to tell her breakfast was being served did she stir.

After breakfast, the morning was taken up with more waiting. This time they queued up at the Port Medical Office for a medical inspection. When her turn came Nora faced a forbidding-looking nurse who had little time for small talk. She asked her questions in an ill-tempered flurry. Nora felt like a dumb animal being examined by a vet as the woman checked her eyes and ears, her hair and continued roughly until she'd reached her feet.

Back at the hotel, the party had dinner and collected their bags for the short walk to the harbour. There, a piper's band greeted them and they boarded a tender called *The Morsecock* which would bring them to where their ship was berthed.

At first she waved happily with the others to the small crowd on the quayside. Then she chanced to look behind her to the other end of the boat and she lowered her waving arm. She had noticed a group of people huddled together with tears streaming down their cheeks. Once in a while they would look back at the town of Cobh where the sun beamed a majestic light on the rows of houses rising from the quays to the hilltop above. She saw the terrible sense of loss in their faces and understood, more than most, how they must feel.

'Are you seasick?' John asked, appearing suddenly beside her. 'You're wicked pale.'

'Sick of you would be more like it,' she answered and moved away wishing that, for once, he would take her more seriously.

All at once a cheer went up and Nora's eyes were drawn seawards.

'There she is,' someone shouted.

'Will you look at the size of it,' another called.

The vast bulk of the SS *Bremen* towered up ahead of their tiny craft. Deep in its shadow, it seemed incredible to Nora that such a colossus of a thing could have been put together by mere men.

Ropes were thrown, ladders lowered and they made their terrifying ascent to the rim of the deck. John was deathly pale as he tried not to look down into the clear depths below.

'I can't stand up on a chair without getting dizzy,' he muttered.

'No need to worry, John,' one of his team-mates called, 'She's as safe as the Titanic!'

'Sweet Lord,' John groaned.

When Nora's feet touched the timbers of the deck she felt the shudder of the engines from somewhere beneath, a shiver of delicious expectation.

A young German deck-hand took her bags and led her to her cabin on deck No. 2. The small space was almost completely taken up with a double bunk and she wondered, a little uneasily, who she would have to share the cabin with. However, it soon became clear that the place would be hers alone for the nine day journey. She was relieved and it didn't occur to her to think why she should have this privilege.

She began to arrange her things neatly on the upper bunk. In the side pockets of one of her bags she discovered a small book-shaped parcel with an envelope attached. She opened it quickly and found a note written in Peter's fine copperplate hand. It said simply, 'Mind yourself and have a good time. Hope you like the book.'

Opening the brown papered parcel she laughed out loud. The book was called *Twenty Thousand Leagues Under The Sea* by Jules Verne. Inside it was inscribed, again in Peter's careful lettering, 'For Nora — Cobh to New York — 10th June 1924.'

She held the book close to her and watched through the porthole as the green land, curiously misshapen as though viewed through a drinking glass, rose and slowly fell. The walls of her cabin began to tremble and, like a giant roused from its slumber, the ship groaned and shook. Its engine's distant roar became a little louder with each passing second. Nora made her way quickly to the top deck where the other passengers had begun to assemble.

In the early evening light the placid waters churned along the sides of the SS *Bremen*.

With a last surge of power the ship moved out towards the unknown. The real journey had begun. Sooner than she'd expected the hills and coastline faded into the blue-white distance behind. She went forward to where she could see the slightly greyer distance ahead.

Between two horizons, the breeze cooling her and the sun warming her, she neither laughed nor cried. The moment was too perfect for simple emotions or words. Only music could come near describing it and her mind was a symphony of sweet confusion.

CHAPTER 3

Nora's descent into sleep that first night on board ship was as smooth and untroubled as the ship's passage between the quiet, dark waves. Through the early night hours the gently rolling sea was like a reassuring whisper in the ears of the sleepers. Then, without warning, it became angry, tossing the ship from side to side.

A sharp knocking noise entered Nora's dreams and refused to go away until eventually she woke. A door rattled on its hinges somewhere nearby. She felt the ship falter in a sinking surge and, just as suddenly, seem to lift her into the air. She sat bolt upright holding on to the sides of the bunk as the falling and rising continued. Waves lashed against the porthole like some strange rain, coming up from below instead of down from above.

She waited in growing horror for the dreaded seasickness Peter had warned her about.

'You'll think you're going to die,' he'd said. 'You might even want to die. All you can do is remember that it'll pass.'

However, instead of feeling unwell she simply began to grow tired again. The swelling sea seemed to find a rhythm that was more comforting than disturbing to Nora. She was soon sleeping as peacefully as before.

When the morning light streaming in by the porthole roused her, all was calm and she was almost convinced she'd merely dreamed the night storm.

Having no idea of the time she dressed and went along the passage towards the dining room. At first she'd imagined it was quite late and that she'd missed breakfast. When she noticed that no one was about she was ready to rush back to her cabin thinking it must be very early. An uneasy feeling came over her as she remembered stories of deserted ships sailing ghost-like, all their passengers disappeared except one, left to roam the eerie decks for eternity.

Then from the dining room up ahead a white-coated steward came into view and called to her in a thick German accent.

'Ach, another one comes.'

As she approached she tried to avert her gaze from this extraordinary man. Though he couldn't have been more than forty, he was completely bald. Not merely closeshaven but totally hairless, right down to the missing eyebrows. The square set of his jaw was granite-like. The muscles of his arms were packed hard inside the sleeves of his perfectly clean jacket. In spite of the impression of toughness, his smile when it broke through the chiselled features was full of an easygoing joviality.

He gave a little bow as she passed quickly by him into the dining room. The place was large and bright and quite empty but for a small group looking very green in the face as they sipped from cups of tea and nibbled uncertainly on thin slices of toast. There was not a sign of John or any of the hurling party. The clock on the wall showed ten o' clock. Nora suddenly felt ravenously hungry but didn't know where she should sit. The steward pulled back a chair for her and handed her a menu.

'Maybe you prefer some tea and the toast,' he said knowingly, 'Such a bad night.'

'I'm kind of hungry,' she told him.

The steward stood back and raised his hairless eyebrows.

'Das ist gut. Very good.'

Nora stared in confusion at the menu with its indecipherable German script. Noticing her discomfort the steward turned the menu around. She turned away to hide her blushes. It was difficult to make a choice with him hovering so close.

'Porridge?' he suggested helpfully.

'Yes.'

'And tea? Toast?' His voice rose in wonder, attracting the attention of the others in the dining room.

This time she didn't even hear what he'd asked but nodded anyway just so he would go away.

With each course of the breakfast another member of the nearby group would jump up and run from the dining room, hands clutching puffed-out cheeks. When she'd finished the last slice of toast she was quite alone except for the white-coated steward. He whisked away the empty plates and bowls, marvelling at her performance.

'Only you and an American in the first class have taken such a breakfast. Small man, big appetite, up there. But you! Biggest appetite on ship.'

As if to prove the old adage about not judging a book by its cover, he turned out to be a very friendly man. He chatted and hummed as he worked and made her feel comfortable in the unfamiliar surroundings. He had introduced himself as Hans Schmeling and told her he was from Berlin. He had a wife and four sons at home and had returned to working at sea after the war. He'd been conscripted into Kaiser Wilhelm's army and fought in France during that terrible world conflict. As he spoke of this Nora saw in his eyes that same troubled look she'd seen in the eyes of men who'd fought in the Civil War.

When she got up to go he shook her hand.

'I enjoy very much our talking,' he said, 'I fed you well on your journey.'

'Thank you, Mr Schmeling.'

'Hans,' he beamed. 'My friends call me Hans.'

It was almost 11.30 when she left the dining room. She decided to go and fetch her book and sit out on the sunny deck for a while. On her way to her cabin she paused at John's door. From inside came a soft, mournful moan that went on for so long it sounded like a chant. This was too good a chance to be missed. She tapped lightly on the cabin door.

'Who is it?' John groaned.

'It's me, Nora.'

'Go away,' he muttered, 'I'm...I'm resting.'

Nora tried the door and found it was unlocked. She peered inside and saw John lying on the floor covered up to his chin with a blanket. Two other men lay stretched out on their bunks. The colour of their faces ranged from pale-grey to a sickly-green. Their eyes were half-closed with only the whites showing.

'Can I do anything for you?' she asked gleefully, 'I could bring you breakfast if you like.'

'Don't mention *food*,' one of the others pleaded.

'Just close the door,' John warned, 'behind you.'

'You can't travel on an empty stomach, you know,' Nora quipped and shutting the door out retreated to her own cabin as quickly as she could. It wasn't long, however, before it dawned on her that John was sleeping on the floor because she was taking up the cabin he should have been sharing with Peter. The fact that she'd taunted him over his seasickness added to her sense of guilt.

The infinitely slow passage of the ship over the following days was a bitter disappointment to her. Each morning after breakfast she would go to the main assembly area where the sailing chart was posted up. Here the progress made each day was announced, along with details of the weather and wind direction. The sea conditions were given too though the passengers already knew these quite well by the condition of their stomachs.

Two hundred and twenty miles they'd travelled on that first day. It had seemed more like twenty. On other days the figure reached three hundred and fifty though it hardly seemed possible so interminably long were the hours. There was so little to do besides sit around. Her life began to centre around the high-ceilinged dining room with its long tables, hum of conversation, clatter of cutlery and din of rattling plates. Life became a matter of passing the time from one meal to the next.

At 8.30 breakfast was served in dining room No. 2. Then there was beef tea on deck at 11. Lunch came at 12.30, followed at 3.30 by tea and finally dinner at 6. After dinner was the worst time. With so little to do but think of eating you seemed to get hungry within an hour of finishing the meal and your stomach was filled with such an emptiness that by morning you were starving again.

Every second day news filtered through from the outside world. *The Ocean Gazette* was a small newspaper printed on board filled mainly with advertisements for hotels, places to see and things to do in New York. Nora read each edition from cover to cover though she had little interest in the news there. The mummy of an ancient Egyptian, Tutankhamun, uncovered; a well-known gangster shot dead in Chicago. In a way it was reassuring that the madness of land-life continued. Perhaps it was healthy to be away from it for a while, even if the means of escape was so boring.

John and the other hurlers soon found their sea-legs and their appetites but he studiously ignored Nora. A typical teaser, he was good at giving it out but not so good at taking it. At twenty-one, she thought, you'd imagine he'd have a bit more sense. It occurred to her that he didn't take her seriously not because he saw her as a child, but because he himself was a child at heart.

He wasn't the only one who behaved like a child. Nora

couldn't understand how the hurlers seemed to change so much aboard ship. They carried on like overgrown boys, playing silly practical jokes on each other, caffling and yelping like the back row messers at her uncle's cinema.

On the fourth day she came upon a group of them gathered around a German deck-hand as he described in gruesome detail the fate of the infamous Titanic on its maiden voyage. She stood a little way off but couldn't keep herself from listening to every word.

Later, she heard that one of the more carefree hurlers had been talking to this deck-hand the day before and he'd got the German to repeat his story so as to frighten the others. The fellow, a big farmer from outside Cashel, thought the whole thing was hilarious. Nora was disgusted at the idea of anyone getting a laugh out of such an awful disaster.

'The night she is as bright as this day. The moon so big. We see the bodies from this very deck,' the German told his rapt, pale audience with a sweep of his tattooed arm. 'We must sail by because of the ice floes. We cannot take them on.'

John Moloney stared out at the gently lapping waves. Nora peered over the rails into the green underwater grave of so many. The deck-hand went on to describe the awesome sights of that fateful night in April 1912, a mere twelve years past. One hundred and fifty bodies they saw, he and his companions.

A man in evening dress laid out on a floating cabin door as if he might, at any moment, sit up and ask for another drink. Two men, arm in arm in death, tossed on the shimmering surface of the sea. Most disturbing of all was the horrifying image of a young woman, her nightdress lit by the moon, a gossamer sail billowing in the icy breeze of the North Atlantic.

The sense of unease was contagious as they listened. Nora imagined the young woman's hopeless struggle against the harsh elements and now every shudder of the SS *Bremen* filled her thoughts with the most terrifying possibilities. She spent the rest of the day on deck. Somehow she felt safer there and as the hours rolled on, the calm sea began to reassert its innocence.

As night fell, and another day had brought them two hundred miles closer to America, Nora stood watching the clear, starry sky. From overhead came the now familiar sound of an orchestra playing in the first class lounge. Some of the hurling party ventured up there from time to time on the invitation of the captain but Nora could never be persuaded.

'With all them pretty German girls around,' John had said, 'you wouldn't get a dance anyway.'

'They'd want to be badly stuck to dance with you,' she'd retaliated.

She wouldn't have minded listening to the music but the thought of being asked to dance by some stranger or worse still by John himself was enough to put her off the idea. The dancing usually finished up at ten o' clock and it was almost that time now. She had been in the habit of going to her cabin as soon as the music stopped but tonight she was feeling more restless than ever. She knew she wouldn't be able to sleep with that woman's image fresh in her mind. And yet the glorious night dulled her fears. The water at once dark and sparkling was like that vision you see when you first close your eyes at night, comforting and restful. She thought of Molly and hoped her blindness, if it should come, might be something like this rather than the deep, all-consuming blackness Nora had imagined it would be.

She moved towards the stern of the ship so that the passengers, drifting back to their cabins, wouldn't see her. Happy voices, among them John's, approached and faded again. Soon the decks were silent and she walked trance-like along them until she found herself at the door of the first class lounge. In all her wanderings around the ship in these last few days it was the one place she'd left unexplored, even when there was no dancing going on. It was, she'd heard, the nicest part of the SS *Bremen*, with plush red velvet seats and curtains and crystal clear-cut lamps.

Now, all but one of these lamps had been extinguished leaving only the orchestra's platform lighted. The dimmer depths of the lounge were splendidly decorated and held rows of finely-polished timber chairs and tables. One day, she dreamed, she would travel in style like this from one continent to the next to perform her music. From New York to Rio De Janeiro to Capetown, Cairo, India, Japan, there would be no limit to her travels only that at the end of each journey there would be a crowded auditorium and a grand piano waiting for her. A grand piano.

Her eyes moved slowly back to the orchestra's empty chairs and on to the darker corner beyond. There, as if it had appeared from thin air, was an unmistakably real grand piano. Its curved top was raised and it looked like a strangely shaped oyster whose pearl was the music waiting to be played. Her fingers tingled as she approached it doubtfully. If she played it would attract attention and probably land her in trouble.

She sat down on the elegant piano stool and opened the lid. If she wasn't meant to play, she thought, the thing would undoubtedly have been locked. It was as good a reason as any to begin. With her foot on the soft pedal she could believe that no one else would hear.

Beginning as always with some scales she quickly realised the notes needed only the merest of touches. The piano she now regarded as her own in Peter's cinema was so different. There, you had to work harder to press down the notes than to actually find them. Here, it was simply a matter of getting your fingers into the right place; the piano seemed to do the rest. She stopped for a moment and listened for the slightest sound.

When she was satisfied that she had disturbed nobody she began to play from memory a piece Alec had sent her from Paris. It was a beautifully haunting piece in three parts, called *Trois Gymnopedies* by Erik Satie. Alec had told her in his letter that he'd met Satie in Paris after the Great War. To Nora, who was used to playing the music of composers who were either long-dead or as impossibly remote as their exotic names, this was overwhelming news. Music was a living thing, made by real people. A thing full of thoughts and emotions that were there to be discovered between the dull lines of notation.

The piece seemed to have been made for this elegant piano. The keys drew her fingers towards them and made the playing almost effortless. She had plenty of time to consider what Alec had said of it.

The three sections, he'd explained, were so alike as to be difficult to tell apart. But differences there were, subtle and effective ones. They'd been described as like walking slowly round a sculpture which though remaining the same in itself seems to change as the angle of your view does.

In her mind, as she played the piece, Nora always imagined a sculpture she'd once seen a photograph of. It portrayed a thin, veiled lady with troubled eyes reaching one arm forward while behind, her right leg was raised slightly but gracefully. Nora would try to decide, as she continued, what that gesture meant.

Was the lady poised for flight and like the Children of Lir about to become a swan? Was she pointing towards something she'd lost or towards something that frightened her? Was it, perhaps, simply a dance and her expression one of concentration rather than fear or doubt? Like the piece itself there was no limit to the possible meanings of the sculpture. As Alec said, the point was not to know but to create the meaning.

She touched out the last A chord, lifted her fingers and almost fell off the stool. There, at the other end of the lounge stood Hans staring across at her. She closed the lid of the piano and began to edge away, certain that her friendship with the steward was finished. He brushed his hand along the top of his head like he had some hair left to smooth down.

'I'm sorry,' she said and headed for the door.

'Come back,' he called.

'I won't do it again.'

'Of course, you must,' he declared, 'Wunderbar.'

'I could have done better if I had the sheet music,' she said, 'I hit a few wrong notes.'

'Better is not possible.'

She left the lounge some time later with an invitation to come and practise any night she wanted to. She told Hans about the piece and her ambitions to be a musician and even a little about how her life had changed course a few years before. He described the misery of the war and the hardships he and his family had been through. They understood each other even when the words were not there to say everything they wanted to say.

'This Molly and Peter,' he'd said, 'I would like to meet. Very good people, yes?'

'Yes, they are,' she agreed, thinking if only she could have said at least that much as they parted at the railway station.

'Ach, many good people,' he sighed, 'but the bad ones have so much to say. Very big their mouths but their hearts? Very small.'

Nora told him too of the unease she'd felt since hearing the deck-hand's story. She wondered if his story hadn't been exaggerated. Hans had to admit that it was all true and told her that he too had seen those bodies adrift on the ice-strewn waters. However, he had words of reassurance for her.

'This *Bremen*, she is not so extravagant, not so arrogant a ship. *Titanic* is too big, too sure of itself. She speeds into icefloes, captain thinks nothing stops me. Then when iceberg hits, so few lifeboats. Even those who build her think, she cannot go down. You cannot charge through like the bull, no one, no thing can. It is the same in all life. No ship can be called "unsinkable", no man cannot fail. Here we take care. Slow but surely, as is said, is our way.'

Nora came to the lounge again the following night and the next. On the third night, however, Hans was too busy to call in so she had the place to herself. She played everything she could think of. Her exam pieces, tunes she'd learned for the cinema, Alec's *Melody for Nora*, until at last, her fingers aching for rest, she returned to Satie's *Gymnopedies* again.

Certain she had never played it so well, she closed the piano lid and drew in a deep breath which should have been released as a sigh of satisfaction. Instead, she froze in horror unable to exhale.

At the small window alongside her she saw the disfigured face of a man, his wide open eyes piercing and fierce in the flawed glass.

CHAPTER 4

The lounge for all its size and grandeur might as well have been half as small again as her tiny cabin, Nora felt so trapped. She didn't dare try the door to the deck. The face had disappeared but she felt certain the stranger was still out there waiting for her. Instead, she lurched across towards the door at the far end, the one Hans used when he came in and out. Where it led she had no idea except that it didn't open on to the deck. She turned the handle but the door wouldn't budge even though she pressed her full weight against it.

'Hans!' she cried and as she did the other door creaked open.

Crouching low beneath the first table she could reach, she saw one dark shoe and then another. When the stranger stood feet apart, just inside the door, she noticed how his long trousers hung in great folds over his shoes. Somehow this made him seem less terrifying and she wondered if the distorted face she'd seen had simply been a trick of the glass. Even in the porthole of her cabin, the glass was not quite clear and seemed to distend the view like rain on a window-pane does. Still, she couldn't bring herself to look up from the neatly polished shoes and the baggy pants.

'Hey, kid,' the stranger called, 'I didn't mean to scare you.'

The voice was strangely muted as if incapable of reaching above a whisper. There was a trace of uncertainty in it too. Nora raised her head slowly above the table-top and forced herself to look directly at him.

What she saw was the quite ordinary face of a middle-aged man whose suit was expensive but ill-fitting. A rich man perhaps who had never got used to being rich. He raised his hat momentarily to reveal a sparse growth of greased-back brown hair. But for his heavy American-accented whisper he might have passed as a bank clerk at the Munster and Leinster Bank on the square at home. His left eye twitched every now and then as harmlessly as a wink.

'Some piano player,' he enthused, screwing his lips into a smile that was more like a grimace. 'I ain't never heard nothing like it.'

Nora moved through the tables and chairs towards him or rather towards the door behind him.

'I should be getting to bed,' she told him as she approached, hoping he would step aside and let her out quickly.

He didn't move. Nora stopped in her tracks.

'Listen, kid,' he said, 'I wanna tell you something. The first night I heard you play here I slept like a baby after. See, I don't sleep too good, not since...since years. That's the truth, I had to come back and listen some more.'

'That's alright,' Nora answered unevenly, 'but I really have to go.'

Still, the stranger didn't show any sign of letting her pass by.

'What's your name? You're Irish, am I right?'

'Nora...Nora Canavan.'

He extended his arm and his hand emerged from the long sleeve of his jacket.

'Vincent...just call me Vincent.'

As she hesitated over whether or not to shake his hand a voice intruded from outside the door behind the stranger.

'You in there, Boss? You OK in there?'

The stranger's face grew dark and his left eye twitched madly. Suddenly he exploded into a fit of rage that sent Nora reeling back among the tables and chairs of the lounge. He turned to the door and without even bothering to open it launched into a tirade of abuse. The man reeked of venom.

'Course I'm OK, you dumb palooka,' he roared. 'Ye think I need a goddam chaperon or what? Get outta here you big lunk before I brain you good and proper.'

'Sorry, Boss,' came the weak reply from the deck.

'Sorry, schmorry. You ain't never around when I need you and when I don't you're up my goddam nose. Go shoot some pool, goonface. Go see if you can figure out which end of the cue hits the ball.'

Nora listened fearfully as the heavy footsteps clumped away and waited for the stranger to turn his frenzied attention to her. He snatched open the door and plunged his clenched fists deep into his trouser pockets, taking a step sideways to clear her passage. She took her chance quickly but as she reached the deck he called quietly after her.

'Sorry 'bout...Sorry,' he muttered. 'It's just 'cause I don't sleep easy. Makes me crazy sometimes.'

She wasn't at all reassured by his soft-spoken words. His uncontrolled anger had made her wonder if violence wasn't perhaps a way of life for the stranger.

'You'll come again tomorrow night, won't you?' he asked.

'I don't...I don't know.'

'Maybe not. Hey, I don't blame you, kid. My wife, my late wife, she always used to say, "Vincent, you got no class." Guess I'll always be a Brooklyn bum, huh?'

'It's very late,' Nora said and walked away, expecting him to yell at her, but the only sound was of the lounge door closing.

As she ran down the steps to No. 2 deck below, she heard single notes being played slowly on the piano as if by a child. In her cabin she lay trembling, frightened by every innocent noise. His gravelly whisper haunted her. 'My late wife.' She couldn't help thinking that his anger had something to do with his wife's death. There was something unspeakably sinister about the contrast between his inoffensive looks and his rough-edged tongue. She would not be returning to the lounge, grand piano or not.

For Nora the last days of the voyage were like a prison sentence. While the hurling party exercised and jogged around the decks to loosen up their cramped limbs, she spent her time in her cabin. When she did emerge it was for a rushed meal followed by a quick dash back to her hideaway again.

John was mystified by her behaviour. In the dining room he noticed how her eyes darted about while she wolfed down her food. Once he followed her out when she'd finished and was bemused to see her running along the deck and ducking into the passage leading to her cabin with a furtive, backward glance. Eventually, he decided to find out what was wrong and went in search of her. When she heard his knock she froze but then his voice came and she was suddenly fuming.

'Nora? I know you're in there.'

'Stop pestering me, will you.'

'Something's up Nora, I know it,' he asserted. 'You're not yourself at all.'

'No, I'm the flippin' Queen of Sheba.'

He didn't answer for a while and she thought disappointedly that he'd gone. When he did speak, she banged her head against the overhead bunk in surprise.

'Did someone say something to you,' he asked, 'or...or do something to you?'

He seemed genuinely concerned and for a moment Nora thought she might actually tell him the truth. If she did she could at least walk around the ship and not be confined in this tiny space all day. John's presence would surely keep the man from approaching her. However, she soon changed her mind.

'Is there some young lad after you?' he joked, meaning only to relieve the tension.

'Go away.'

'No, really, Nora,' he said, 'I'm serious now, if there's someone bothering you, apart from myself of course, I'll deal with them. I mean it now, honest.'

Nora stared miserably out of the porthole at the bright day.

'I mean to say,' John tried once more, 'I'm a guard, like. I'd know how to handle it.'

'Some guard you are. You couldn't catch a cold.'

'I don't understand why you always make so little of me, Nora,' he said quietly and she was too astonished at the tremor in his voice to react.

She lay back trying not to think about him and wishing the hours away. She tried to imagine the scene at New York harbour when she'd meet her brothers but the shadow of the stranger would not pass. Even when she concentrated her mind on his ridiculously large suit and his miserable apologies it made her feel no better. She kept returning to his sudden charge of temper that had shot through her like a bolt of lightning. It sent shivers down her spine even yet.

At dinner that evening she ate in her usual mad scramble. Hans was clearly startled by her new coldness towards him but Nora didn't have time to notice as she kept her eyes on the dining room door and the windows to the deck. She had barely been sitting down five minutes when she was ready to leave again. Before she did, Hans came to her table.

'You have a problem, fraulein?' he asked. 'Always in the big hurry now.'

'I don't feel well.'

'But you eat more than ever. And so quickly. Not good.'

She couldn't bring herself to tell him to mind his own business as she'd done with John. Instead, she shrugged her shoulders.

'And the music? You don't come to play, why?'

How could she explain that she was afraid of some

stranger who'd complimented her and lost his temper with another stranger she hadn't even seen? It was too ridiculous. She stood up and ran from the dining room leaving the bewildered steward to pick up the chair she'd knocked over. He looked dumbstruck around the room as if to ask if anyone knew what had gotten into Nora. From the kitchen someone called his name and he retreated there, wondering what he'd done to the girl he had come to regard almost as the daughter he'd never had.

After this incident Hans didn't serve at her table any more from fear that he would upset her again. Nora hadn't felt so friendless since her first days in Tipperary. She ached to be in New York and silently cursed the slow, cumbersome progress of the SS *Bremen*. So unhappy and ashamed did she feel that on the last night of the journey she didn't even bother to go to the dining room for the evening meal. It was to be a special farewell banquet but even that prospect didn't tempt Nora to release herself from her solitary confinement.

She listened to the distant strains of the orchestra and the excited hum of the passengers all around her. It seemed as though the whole ship had come alive in anticipation of the journey's end. The humdrum days of the passage were forgotten in the celebrations but for Nora another night of broken sleep beckoned.

Tonight, at least there was the packing to do and she took her time with this, folding everything slowly and carefully and convincing herself that things were not as bad as she'd let herself imagine. She filled the wash-basin and began to wash her hair, humming softly all the while. Only one more night on the ship, she thought. Even if it proved to be a long, sleepless one it was still the last. She felt reassured, comforted by the pleasant tingling of warm water on her scalp and began to sing out with more confidence. For a while her singing drowned out the persistent rapping on her cabin door.

Finishing her song on a high note she was already deciding what to sing next when she heard the stranger's coarse whisper. It was too late, she knew, to pretend she wasn't in.

'Can we talk, kid?'

'I'm...I'm in bed,' she cried falteringly.

'It's important,' he implored. 'I got a proposition for you. On the level, kid.'

Water dripped from her hair on to the shoulders of her dress but she hardly noticed.

'I know I scared you but I want to make up for it, see. I don't mean you no harm. On my wife's grave, I swear it.'

The hair on Nora's neck bristled but by now she was as curious as she was fearful.

'Just hear me out,' he pleaded.

'I'm listening.'

'Open the door, kid. I ain't gonna jump you.'

She drew the door back just enough to see him. He was wearing a different suit. It was as new and as poor a fit as the other one he'd worn. His fingers fidgeted uneasily with the hat he'd swept off his head when she'd appeared.

'You been sick?' he asked. 'I ain't seen you round the place for a while.'

'Yes,' she lied.

'But you're OK now. I mean you look fine.'

'What do you want from me?' she asked testily.

'I'll come to the point,' he said and she could sense his disappointment at her unfriendliness. 'I been thinking about you and the piano and like I said before, I ain't never heard nothing like it from a...well, from such a young kid. Not saying I'm no expert or nothing but hey, if you can put me to sleep then you gotta be good.'

She stared at him fixedly.

'Joke, kid,' he explained. 'Anyways, I'll get to the point. You really can play and I can help you. See, I happen to know a guy who runs this big music academy in New York. My late wife was like a benefactor, you know. That is, she gave this academy lots of dough, my dough, but, hey, she had good reasons, we both had.'

He looked at Nora for some response but there was none.

'But getting to the point, he owes me plenty favours and, hey, listen, in case you think different, we're not talking some small-time outfit here. This is the number one academy, the best that money can buy. And, well, I want to send you there, pay the fees, your keep, everything. But I want to do this right, you know. Parents' permission and all that stuff. I mean I ain't trying to kidnap you now or nothing. On the level.'

Nora's mouth hung open and she'd forgotten completely to keep the door from swinging back. The shoulders of her dress were now saturated with water from her hair. The breeze coming in from the passage felt like ice passing through her shoulder blades.

'You don't have to decide right away,' he said, 'think about it for a while, maybe you...'

Just then a commotion started up nearby. The stranger looked back to where the thudding sounds came from. At first Nora thought someone had locked themselves into their cabin and was trying to attract attention by banging on their door. Soon, however, she heard two familiar voices.

'Take a hike, mister,' the stranger's friend was warning. 'You can't come by here until the Boss is finished talking, see.'

'I am an officer of this ship,' Hans replied, 'You have no right to give me the orders.'

'Get outa here, Kaiser.'

'Nora?' Hans called, 'These men, they are troubling you?'

She looked at the stranger. His face was clouding over again in that particular way it had done before his outburst in the lounge.

'No,' she replied, 'It's just a silly mistake. This man called to the wrong cabin.'

The stranger seemed relieved.

'Sure,' he said, 'My mistake.'

He leaned towards her and whispered.

'You'll think about it?'

'I have thought about it,' she told him, 'and I'm not interested...but thanks anyway.'

She closed the cabin door and left him standing outside. After a few moments she heard him call to his partner from some way off.

'You scared her off, you dummy. I mighta convinced her.'

She looked at her hands and saw that she was trembling. Looking in the mirror she realised how pale she'd grown beneath the wet strings of hair hanging witch-like over her face. She began to dry her hair, barely able to lift the towel to her head. The door was tapped lightly.

'Nora.'

It was Hans. She let him in and in a sudden rush of words she told him everything that had happened. He listened patiently until she became calm.

'We will make very sure,' he promised her, 'that these people do not bother you again.'

'But how?'

'Ach, there are but two of them,' he smiled, 'and many of us in our crew. We will say very politely they must not disturb you. These are not good men, these Americans. The big one, he has the gun. In my struggle I felt it in his jacket.'

Nora gasped and began to shake again.

'Nothing to worry you, Nora,' he reassured her and from his white coat he produced a pistol. 'Perhaps, I make a better pickpocket than sailor, no? Now, you must sleep. Tomorrow morning, very early, it will be New York.'

Hans left with a grin, touching the pocket where the gun was hidden.

'Our big friend will not feel so big now.'

All night her eyes never closed for more than a few minutes. The sea was calm but her mind was tossed upon waves of fear, doubt and anticipation. In spite of all that had happened it was the excitement of the next day that won out in the end.

In dawn's early light she saw, at last, the brightly-lit outline of New York harbour. She felt so good it was like the relief of walking from a nightmare she believed had passed forever.

CHAPTER 5

Nora stood hidden among the group of hurlers on the upper deck of the tender taking them from the SS *Bremen* to Hoboken Pier. It had been a hectic morning. She had met Hans to thank him for all he'd done and to apologise again for the days of silence, and was delighted to hear that they'd meet again on the return journey. They lined up for yet another medical check and again to have their passports stamped. All the while, Nora watched for the stranger and his henchman but they were nowhere to be seen. Now that the shoreline loomed up ahead, her dread of them was fading quickly. The sights and sounds all around were so over-whelming there was no place in her mind for anything but sheer wonder.

The tall, jagged skyline of buildings stretched as far as the eye could see. Here, in the harbour, there were so many crafts of all shapes and sizes it hardly seemed possible that the tender could chart a course between them. Even the faces of those for whom there would be no return home were lit up by the extraordinary scene.

Soon they were within earshot of the crowds and the tender slowly arched around until it came alongside the dock. Nora couldn't see her brothers in the throng below and if they called to her their voices were sure to be lost in the din.

John stayed close but didn't say anything. Perhaps it was

the exciting atmosphere, the spectacular feeling of optimism and hope but whatever the reason Nora actually wanted him to speak to her. Somehow, she felt, his silence wasn't born out of any malice towards her. She had the distinct impression that he had something important to tell her but couldn't quite bring himself to.

The passengers began to stream down on to the dockside and one by one they were swallowed up in the mêlée below. John, trailing a little behind Nora, turned to answer someone's call and when he looked back towards the dock again, she had disappeared. She was too busy, searching among the faces around her for the boys, to notice.

People of every colour surrounded her. A chorus of languages assailed her ears, some curiously high-pitched, others deep and brooding. Men in peaked caps tried to grab her bags but she held on to them as they swapped suspicious looks with her.

She was becoming so desperate that she turned to look for John but he too was lost in the crowd. Then she thought of the stranger and had a sudden vision of being abducted by him and his friend. If such a thing happened, who would notice in this whirlwind of humanity? Someone tapped her shoulder. She almost screamed.

'I thought you were lost, girl,' John said, the sweat pouring from his forehead.

'I was.'

'Follow me, and we'll see if we can find your uncle.'

'Some chance,' she sneered, but made sure to keep up with him just the same.

Ten minutes later they both stood perplexed at the edge of the rapidly-thinning crowd.

'Are you sure they know it's today you're coming?'

'Peter wrote to him. He must know.'

'I'm supposed to be marching to the City Hall with the

team,' he told her, looking at his watch.

'Go on off so,' she said sourly, 'You're not doing much good here anyway.'

'Jaykers,' he cried in exasperation, 'I can't make them appear out of thin air, you know. I'm not a flippin' magician.'

'What's wrong with you today?' she asked, 'You're like an anti-Christ.'

'Nothing,' he muttered and looked distractedly in the direction of the tender they'd just left.

Her eyes followed his and she saw something he didn't notice. The stranger and his muscular shadow walked quickly down the gangplank, with their coat collars turned up and the peaks of their hats covering their eyes. Immediately, they were surrounded by an advancing horde of photographers, reporters and policemen. She couldn't hear what was being said but her eyes met the stranger's for a brief instant and his lips formed a faint smile. It seemed to her like a smile of apology and regret. He was gone before she could decide how to respond.

'Nora,' John whispered, 'There's two young fellows over there with a tall thin chap. Would that...?'

'Ritchie!' she shouted, 'Denis!'

Even from a distance of thirty yards she could see how much they'd grown. They were no longer the pudgy little boys she'd known. Denis was still the taller of the two but now, a few months short of their eleventh birthday, it was a matter of a mere few inches. Their hair stood in wavy mops. Ritchie's was more blonde than red now. Denis, on the other hand, was as dark-haired as ever. Between them stood Uncle Phil, lean and handsome in his brown leather jacket and soft cap, waving to her excitedly.

Ritchie was the first to reach her. He threw his arms around her and she could feel the sobs he was trying to hold back shake through her. She held him as tight as a mother's embrace. When he let her go, Denis was standing before her. He was staring at her so hard she was taken aback. Then his face broke into a grin and he stuck out his hand towards her.

'How you was, Nora,' he said.

She took his hand in some confusion.

'It means, "How're you gettin' on",' Ritchie explained, throwing his eyes up to heaven. 'Denis likes to talk like a real American.'

'Ah, take a hike, Ritchie,' and though he laughed as he spoke, Nora felt a chill run down her spine remembering where she'd heard that phrase before — on board the SS *Bremen* the previous night.

'Give your sister a good, decent hug, Denis,' Phil told him.

Denis blushed uneasily as he embraced her. This time it was Nora who had to stifle the emotion welling up inside her.

'Sorry we're so late. I got delayed at work,' Phil explained.

'I thought you'd never get here,' John said, shaking Phil's hand. 'John Moloney's the name.'

'You scored five points in the All-Ireland Final last year, right?' Phil recollected. 'It's an honour to meet you.'

'I was lucky,' John beamed, 'The fellow marking me had only the one leg.'

'He must have been blind too,' Nora suggested, annoyed at the childish pleasure he was taking in being recognised, annoyed too that he hadn't said whatever it was that was on his mind earlier. Suddenly she thought of Molly and immediately regretted her words.

'Here, I'd better go before she starts kissing me goodbye.'

'You got a soft spot for John, do you?' Phil declared.

'He's the one with the soft spot,' she snapped, 'on the brain.'

John offered his hand hesitantly to Nora and she gave him a cold, limp handshake.

'Nora, in case I don't see...' he stuttered and then in a

sudden embarrassed rush said, 'Be careful and have a nice time.'

'I will now,' she said but her heart was racing wildly.

Phil took her bags and the boys linked arms with her as they made their way through the dockers busily unloading cargo from every end of the earth. She had imagined that when she met Denis and Ritchie all three of them would be talking non-stop. In reality, it was difficult to think of the right things to say and their conversation was polite and hesitant. If it hadn't been for Phil the long pauses might have become unbearable. He asked her about the journey and about how things were back in Ireland. He told her how well the boys were doing at school and how good they were at helping around the house. The kind of small talk that smoothes the way through the awkwardness that was natural in the circumstances.

Nora was surprised at how little Phil had changed from that photograph taken so long before. His face was still boyish if a trifle more scored with worry lines. He was darker than her father but the resemblance was unmistakable. When she looked from him to the boys she could see that they could easily have been taken for his sons. This was especially true of Denis with his sallow features and jet-black hair.

'Why don't we take a cab,' enquired Phil, 'and show Nora the sights?'

This was obviously as much a treat for her brothers as it was for her. Denis and Ritchie ran ahead and vied with each other to hail one of the yellow-painted taxis on the street. Denis seemed to move like lightning, leaving his brother trailing awkwardly behind. Watching this amusing little contrast Nora could believe they hadn't changed much after all. It almost seemed like they were back in Inchicore again and she had to stop herself from calling out to them in the fussy way she had then, to stop the messing. Instead, she just laughed, feeling easy in herself again.

'Never a dull moment with these guys, I can tell you,' Phil said and then shouted good-humouredly at the boys, 'One cab is enough.'

As the taxi wound its way into the heart of the city, Nora was astounded by the sheer scale of the buildings on all sides. On the pavements, the pedestrians seemed to have some-where to go that was very important, they walked so quickly and purposefully. The heat, once they'd left the open, breezy spaces of the port, made her whole body tingle. The open cab windows let in a clamour of noise from car horns, the whistles of traffic police, the virtual thunder of thousands of footsteps and a cacophony of voices arguing, laughing and talking loudly in the busy swelter. It was if humanity had to make a gigantic, bellowing effort to be heard or seen in the brick and concrete valleys of the city.

Only the traffic moved slowly amid the chaotic scene. Lights were already being switched on everywhere when they left the busier streets and drove into others whose scale was more familiar. By now, the prickly heat had become very uncomfortable. Nora's clothes were damp with perspiration and her feet swollen despite the new shoes. Ritchie and Denis didn't seem bothered by the clammy atmosphere. They were busy pointing out this landmark and that and Nora did her best to appear as enthusiastic as they were.

'This is the Bronx,' Denis said. 'We're nearly home.'

Home. The word came so naturally to his lips that Nora felt a sinking sensation. Somehow it left her feeling excluded, an outsider who might well have been a second or third cousin rather than a sister to the boys.

'Phil, wake up,' Ritchie cried, 'We're in Mott Haven.'

Only now did Nora notice that Phil had fallen asleep in the front seat of the cab. He stirred himself and stretched his arms over his head.

'To sleep perchance to dream,' he declared grandly.

'He's doin' it again,' Ritchie groaned, 'The Bronx Poet.'

'That's William Shakespeare actually,' Phil told him. 'These guys have no appreciation of the finer things in life, Nora.'

'Phil swallowed a dictionary when he was a kid,' Denis whooped.

'Second left up here,' Phil told the cab-driver, ignoring the insults from behind.

They had turned into a street of three-storey, brownstone houses. At the corner was a shop with large red lettering across its window proclaiming, 'Wash-Basin Grocery Store'. It struck Nora as a most peculiar name. Wash-Basin was surely not someone's name and whoever heard of a grocery store selling wash-basins? Then again, this was such an extraordinary city that anything was possible here. Further down on the right-hand side was a rather grand, if faded, building of grey stone with wide sweeping steps leading to a portico of Romanesque columns. It looked altogether out of place among the sober houses of the street.

The cab pulled up and while Phil paid the fare, the boys got her bags and led her up the railed steps to the front door. She was surprised at how large the house was and wondered why the boys shared a bedroom — there must have been at least six or seven bedrooms in this place.

Phil joined them at the door and took out a bunch of keys. Ritchie and Denis jostled each other playfully to be first in behind their uncle.

'D'ye think you'll be able to put up with these guys for four weeks?' he grinned.

'I'm supposed to be staying five weeks,' Nora said hesitantly. 'Didn't Peter tell you when he wrote?'

'Oh, right, I musta got confused,' Phil exclaimed, the pitch of his voice strangely high.

'I can't believe it, Phil,' Ritchie beamed, 'She's got a whole extra week with us.'

'Yeah,' Phil said, regaining his composure, 'That's...that's just swell.'

He found the right key at last and they stepped inside the front door. The huge sense of growing unease of these last few days returned all at once as the heavy door shuddered on its hinges and closed.

CHAPTER 6

Nora followed apprehensively as Phil and her brothers climbed the first flight of stairs from the wide hallway. She had expected to be led into one of the ground floor rooms. However, of the three doors she saw there, one hung crookedly from its hinges and the others were nailed up with heavy planks of timber.

By the time they'd reached the top of the house, the truth had dawned on her. This was an apartment building and her uncle a mere tenant of the top floor.

The staircase was rickety and creaked beneath them as they passed up. On the walls was a thickly embossed wallpaper painted over in a sickly green colour. There were spots where the paper curled at the edges like the pages of an old book left out for too long under the sun. It took all the strength she could muster to hide her disappointment and concern that the boys had to live in such a run-down place.

She had expected to be greeted by Phil's wife, Fay, when they stepped into the dark apartment. Instead, there was only a humid silence.

'Let's open some windows, guys,' Phil said, flicking on the light switch.

The stark electric light, so different from the comfortable glow of the oil lamps in Stannix Lane, stung her eyes. The room was not as small as she'd imaged in the moment before the light came on. Neither was it as forbidding as the musty green stairwell. Cheerfully decorated walls were hung on all sides with drawings in polished frames. A long window, wide as a gate and reaching almost to the floor, looked out on to the street below. Everywhere there were books, on shelves or stacked in untidy piles in the corners of the room.

Denis pulled a cloth from a table in the middle of the room and Nora looked around in surprise at the rest of the furniture. Each piece was covered with a similar cream-coloured sheet.

'It's the sun,' Denis explained, holding up one of the sheets. 'Things get faded if you don't cover them.'

Phil and Ritchie were going through the other rooms, opening windows and chatting away non-stop.

'Where's Fay?' Nora asked of Denis.

'She'll be back soon. I gotta check the mailbox.'

It was clear he didn't want to talk to her. Ritchie burst into the room as Denis disappeared onto the landing outside. He noticed her troubled look as she stared at the half-open door.

'Take off your coat,' he said, 'and make yourself at home. Phil's getting the dinner. Bet you're starving.'

'Denis hasn't much to say, has he?'

'Ah, he doesn't talk to nobody much, 'cept maybe Fay.'

'Doesn't talk to anybody, you mean,' Nora corrected him.

'Sorry,' Ritchie said sheepishly.

'Don't mind me,' she apologised, 'I shouldn't be acting the big sister.'

'Why not? You still are my big sister.'

She peeled off her coat and Ritchie took it. From the next room the smell of food wafted in but Nora wasn't hungry. Ritchie opened a long press to hang the coat in and an assortment of boxes and shoes tumbled to the floor around his feet.

'Fay's been tidying up again,' he laughed.

Nora's mother had gone out to work when times were hard back in Inchicore and Molly too worked every hour in the shop as well as in the home. This was different. Both Molly and her mother, at least until her final illness began, had been able to keep their homes running smoothly in spite of the other jobs they had to take on. From the evidence so far, Fay was unable to do so. Nora wondered if her neglect extended to her care for the boys.

At the same time she realised she was falling into an age-old trap. How often had she heard her mother say that when people walked into a dirty home they would invariably blame the woman of the house, never the husband or the sons. She was angry with herself and yet she couldn't help turning this anger on Fay, a woman she'd never even laid eyes on.

'Where is she anyway?' she asked.

'She works three hours a day,' Ritchie explained brightly, 'down Broadway. In a flower shop.'

'And who takes care of you when she's out?'

Leaving the boys alone for a few hours in Inchicore was one thing, doing so in New York was surely irresponsible, she thought.

'She don't...she doesn't have to go until Phil gets back from the bank.'

Nora eyed him suspiciously. This was the first she'd heard of Phil's working in a bank. In fact, when she thought about it she realised they'd never mentioned anything in their letters about what he did for a living. There was obviously a lot more they hadn't told her. She wondered if they'd been warned not to say anything in their letters except that they were well and happy in their new home.

'How come he doesn't dress like a bank clerk?'

Ritchie stood up with a bundle of socks in his hands. He gave her a quizzical look and then smiled. 'He's not a bank clerk. He's a security guard.'

A security guard in a city like this where bank raids, she

imagined, were a daily occurrence. What would happen to
the boys if, having lost their mother and father, they should
lose Phil too?

'But he doesn't have a uniform,' Nora said in disbelief.

'Sure he does. He changes before he leaves the bank so no
one can follow him and find out where he lives.'

Nora sat heavily into a chair, astonished at the precarious
situation her brothers had found themselves in.

'Why would anyone want to know where he lives?'

'So they could make him help them rob the bank, of
course,' Ritchie said cheerfully.

'Doesn't it worry you that he might be...be killed or...'

'Naw, Phil's real tough. He stopped four guys robbing the bank
a while back. Got his ribs busted in but they didn't get a dime.'

He put away the last of the boxes and closed the long press.
Now that she was sitting down, Nora felt desperately tired.
So much had happened since her last sleepless night on board
the SS *Bremen* and with every minute her tiredness was
driving her to a new pitch of distraction. She needed to clear
her head and she knew that sleep was the only answer. Then
again, how could she sleep with so many things bothering
her? She closed her eyes and felt the room rise and fall slowly
as if she was still on the ship. Tiny beads of perspiration
showed clearly on her forehead under the harsh electric light.
From the bottom of the stairs she heard Denis call.

'Fay's here.'

Then, more faintly, she heard a woman's voice, though it
sounded more like the voice of a young girl.

'How you was, sugar.'

They were coming up the stairs now and it seemed that
Denis' tongue had been loosened from whatever it was that
tied it up in Nora's presence.

'We went and picked up Nora at Hoboken,' he told Fay,
'She's lookin' great.'

'All the Canavans look good to me, sweetheart,' the woman giggled.

They were very close by now. Fay's perfume had reached the room before her. Nora could hear Denis chuckling just outside the door. She sat up rigidly in her chair.

'You feelin' alright, Fay?' Denis wondered.

'What 'ye mean, do I feel alright?'

'Cause the place is real neat in here,' he sniggered. 'Did you pay someone to do it?'

'Watch it, kiddo,' Fay exclaimed in mock horror.

Denis ducked in the door of the apartment with Fay in pursuit. They were like two children, like brother and sister the way they carried on.

'This is Auntie Fay,' Denis declared as he lurched across to the other side of the table from her.

'Auntie,' Fay grimaced, 'He calls me that just to annoy me. Now, who's gonna do the introductions?'

'Nora, this is Fay,' Ritchie said, 'Fay, this is our sister, Nora.'

'It's a real pleasure to meet you. I've heard so much about you,' Fay said with a little bow.

Nora hesitated, unable to stir herself. She stared at the woman who seemed impossibly young to be anyone's aunt. Perhaps, she thought, it was simply that the heavy make-up and the stylish clothes masked the years. Fay had all the glamour of the screen heroines Nora had so often seen and somehow didn't belong in this small apartment. Whatever role she was suited to, the part of a mother was certainly not the one that came to mind.

'Thank you for having me,' Nora said, forcing herself to be pleasant.

Fay came and sat beside her. She took Nora's hand and looked into her eyes with her easy smile.

'I hope you'll be happy with us. Maybe you'll teach these guys some manners.'

Nora released her hand from Fay's grasp. Her eyes smarted as the perspiration trickled under her eyelids. Fay glossed gracefully over the sharp silence. The nerve of this woman to talk about her brothers' manners. There was nothing wrong with their manners before they left Dublin, she thought.

'Must be the city,' Fay said, 'Nobody's got time for manners in a city, I guess.'

Nora wondered if Fay was deliberately trying to provoke. With great effort she stopped herself from saying that Dublin was a city too. It seemed to her that every thought she had now was more petty than the one before. Life was different here. If she didn't get used to that fact, her holiday would be miserable from beginning to end. Peter had warned her not to expect that people lived in the same way all the world over but even he, she was sure, would have been disturbed by what he found here.

Phil appeared at the door leading to the kitchen. By now Nora wasn't up to feeling surprised anymore even though he stood there in his trousers and sleeveless vest. He'd taken off his shirt, shoes and socks.

'Anyone feel like a bite to eat?'

Fay slipped off her shoes and padded gracefully across to him. There, in full view of the boys and Nora, she kissed him and Ritchie let out a groan. 'Yyyyyuuukkkk.'

Denis whistled loudly and started singing, trying to deepen his voice. 'Like a hand in a glove, like a foot in a shoe, we fit together, doobie-do-doo.'

Everyone laughed except Nora. She'd never seen husbands and wives acting like this before. It was more than ridiculous. There was something showy about it as if they were trying to prove they loved each other. As if they weren't quite sure themselves and had to act out the part to convince themselves and everyone else.

Ritchie and Denis dashed into the kitchen.

'Last in is a dumb cluck,' Denis shouted, winning as usual.

'Get back out here, you guys,' Fay called, 'and wash those hands.'

They trailed out sheepishly to the landing and Nora heard the sound of running water. Phil returned to the kitchen leaving Nora alone with Fay.

'So, how's tricks in the Emerald Isle?'

'Fine,' Nora answered coldly.

'And your folks...Molly and Peter, I mean?'

'Fine.'

'How about your dad?' Fay tried again. 'Phil worries about him, lots.'

Nora was taken aback at how freely Fay spoke with her. She didn't like it one bit. None of your flippin' business, was what she felt like saying.

'There's nothing to be worried over,' she said instead, and feeling obliged to defend her father's seeming desertion of them, added, 'He did what he thought was best.'

'Course he did,' Fay said, taking Nora's hand in that annoying way again. If she was trying to be sarcastic her innocent look of sympathy masked it well. Nora was painfully aware that for all her revoltingly fancy ways, Fay was the only one who'd bothered to ask after her father. It was, she knew, unreasonable but that fact made her even more suspicious of her aunt.

Ritchie and Denis passed back to the kitchen, scuffling noisily.

'Would you like to freshen up before you eat?' she asked, 'I'll show you the ladies' room. Well, it's actually the men's room too. We ain't so fancy.'

She led the way to the landing and to a door next to the one they'd just come through. Back at home in Tipperary, the toilet was in an outhouse in the yard, you used the jug and yewer in your room to wash and at weekends, you had a bath in a steel tub filled with kettles of boiling water from the warm range. Here, everything was neatly arranged together in one room like in some grand hotel.

Fay closed out the door behind her and Nora, alone at last, threw cold water on her face. She looked in the mirror and didn't like what she saw. Her wiry hair was a mess and her cheeks glowed a bright red. She tried more cold water and sat on the side of the bath waiting to cool down, inside and out.

'Hey, Nora,' Ritchie called, 'are you asleep in there or what?'

'Coming,' Nora said, jumping to her feet and wondering if she really had nodded off.

'Your dinner will be cold.'

Nora snapped open the door and pulled Ritchie inside. He fell back against the wall, stiffening up like he was being attacked by some stranger.

'Tell me the truth, Ritchie,' she whispered, 'Do you really like living in this...this tenement?'

'This is no tenement,' Ritchie objected. 'We got everything here. Running water, electricity and...'

'The truth.'

'You makin' me out a liar?' He backed away from her towards the half-open door. 'Your dinner...will be cold.'

'Why are all the rooms barred up in this house?' she wanted to know.

'It's nothing, Nora, only the guy who owns the place is selling up and he's got to have everyone out before anyone'll buy it.'

'So, you could all be out on the street at any minute.'

'No, it's not like that. We got three months to find a new apartment. Phil's been looking around already. It won't be a problem, you got it all wrong.'

He turned away from her and walked uncertainly back into the apartment. At the door he stopped and faced her again.

'I don' understand why...' he began, 'Why you have to be so...so...'

'Ritchie, I'm sorry,' she moaned, her head spinning violently, 'I'm not always like this...I feel like I'm cracking up.'

Ritchie went into the apartment and she stared at the hideous wallpaper. The last thing in the world she wanted to do right now was to follow him inside. She looked down the rotting stairs but it led only to an unfamiliar street in a bewildering city. There was no choice, nowhere to hide.

Closing the apartment door behind her she heard Ritchie's voice from the kitchen.

'She's all upset. I don't know why.'

The tension in the air seemed almost to cling to her, burning through to her very fingertips.

CHAPTER 7

When Nora reached the kitchen a too obviously light-hearted conversation was underway. They turned and smiled at her as she entered and she wondered if it was possible she'd only imagined what Ritchie had said. Her head was filled with a curious echo as she sat down and for fully five minutes she watched their mouths moving but could make no sense of their words.

The heady mixture of accents didn't help either — the boys' familiar Dublin drawl lifted once in a while by an American twang; Phil's 'Noo Yawk' patter interspersed with Dublin strains; Fay's mile-a-minute banter.

She felt miserably self-conscious, sure that her face was an ugly crimson compared to Fay's delicately painted pallor. The meat on her plate was covered with a spicy red sauce that seemed to make her sweat even more with every mouthful. She drank glass after glass of water and felt a horrendous swelling sensation in her stomach. Fay ate only a slice of toast and her perfect slimness made Nora feel positively obese.

Someone had closed the kitchen window before she'd come in and she wanted to ask the boys to open it but couldn't. Even on winter nights the kitchen at Stannix Lane, its metal range crackling with the heat from piles of turf, was never as hot as this. Here was a heat without warmth, a heat that brought no comfort. Missing too were the homely pots and pans hanging on racks by the window, the open dresser lined with earthenware crockery. Here everything was light and insubstantial, nothing was made to last, not these plates or the tiny cooking dishes or the frail, yellow-painted shelves they stood upon.

The cooker was a gleaming white but ridiculously small and evil-smelling gas affair. A little electric gadget boiled the water and another popped up slices of unevenly toasted bread. As far as Nora could see, when she'd got over her surprise at these things, they all added up to a recipe for pure laziness.

Though Fay could not have understood why, Nora asked rather pointedly if she could help her wash the dishes. Fay insisted that Nora was on 'vacation' and wouldn't dream of letting her so much as wash a cup. Phil checked his watch and, standing up quickly, announced: 'Time for a bit of song and dance.'

Nora looked askance at him.

'The radio,' he explained and led her to the sitting room. Ritchie followed but Denis stayed in the kitchen clearing off the table with Fay. Phil whisked away yet another slip-cover to reveal an elegantly carved wooden box-like object, square on the bottom and rounded on top with a row of black knobs on its front. The only radio Nora had ever seen was a peculiar cylinder-shaped thing one of the neighbours at home had made. The voices and music coming from it had been so impossibly faint he'd had to explain he was still working on it.

'My pride and joy,' Phil exclaimed. 'Only talks when I want it to. Not like the rest of this crowd.'

When he turned one of the knobs Nora was stunned by how clear the woman's voice was, like she was in the room with them.

Her uncle began to fiddle with another of the knobs and snatches of music and speech came and went between blasts of whistling noises.

'Aw, Phil,' Ritchie complained, 'You're not listening to that old mush again, are you?'

'You got no taste, kid,' Phil grinned, 'The man that hath no music in himself, is fit for treasons, stratagems and spoils.'

'But I wanna tune into the serial on WJZeee. And Nora don't wanna hear that old wailin'.'

Phil turned to Nora and she shrugged her shoulders wondering what all this 'mush' and 'wailing' was in the first place.

Now a male voice was reading the news, and picking a book from one of the careless heaps, Phil went and sat by the window. Ritchie looked at his sister and threw his eyes up to heaven.

The news ended and another voice introduced itself.

'This is Jim Carter on Station WLWL,' he announced. 'Right now we have something special for all you Irish folks out there. It's the *Hour of Irish Songs and Music*, with Nell O'Brien, soprano and Bryan Kilpatrick, tenor; accompanied by the Emerald Instrumental Trio.'

As the radio programme went on Nora detected a raw, scraping edge to what had, at first, seemed like a perfect replica of real sound. The electric light too was utterly different from the gentle gaslight of home. Together these things created an air of unreality and falseness.

Phil lowered his eyes and seemed to be reading intensely as he listened. Before the programme had ended she realised that he had, in fact, fallen asleep. Denis joined them from the kitchen and went over to where his uncle sat, unable to disguise a concerned frown.

'We should wake him,' Ritchie whispered.

'Give him a few more minutes,' Denis said, 'He's flat out.'

Fay breezed in brightly, a tea towel in one hand and a dripping cup in the other.

'Phil,' she called, 'You're gonna be late for work.'

He jumped to his feet and looked around as if he'd forgotten momentarily where he was. He glanced at his watch and let out a groan.

'Why didn't you wake me earlier?' he cried.

Denis went and fetched his uncle's jacket and cap. Ritchie dashed into the kitchen and returned with a small box.

'Here's your sandwiches.'

'Anyone seen my torch?'

'I put it in your pocket.'

'Sorry 'bout having to rush off like this, Nora,' her uncle said and kissing Fay on the cheek he lumbered across to the apartment door, taking a book from the shelves on his way.

'I know you got a lot to talk about, kids,' he said, 'but don't stay up too late, right.'

The door closed and he was gone. Nora searched among their faces for an explanation but none came. On the radio an orchestra was playing a loud, pompous piece that grated on Nora's ears.

'Can we switch over to something else?' Denis wondered.

'Sure,' Fay said, 'Go ahead. That's pretty awful stuff, huh, Nora.'

'It's not too bad,' Nora replied, unwilling to let herself agree with her aunt on anything.

'Pity we don't have a piano. I hear you're a real wiz on the ivories. Maybe...'

'Does Phil have to work late at the bank?' Nora asked sharply.

Ritchie and Denis were fighting over which station to listen to. Behind them, Nora and Fay stood at opposite ends of the table as if preparing for a duel. Nora felt so tired she was sure her eyes were about to pop out. Beneath her aunt's long eyelashes she detected a fleeting glint of steel.

'He's got a second job down at a warehouse, couple of nights a week,' Fay said evenly. 'It's not unusual, not in this city. Life is tough here. Everything costs.'

'He seems so...tired.'

'Damn right he's tired, you don't need to tell *me* that.'

Nora didn't know what to say next. She'd already said too much. She felt queasy and couldn't decide whether to sit down or make some excuse about having to go to the bathroom.

'Maybe we're all a tad tired tonight?' Fay ventured. 'I think we should all hit the sack.'

'But it's early,' Ritchie whined.

Denis dug his elbow into Ritchie's side and nodded towards the long couch by the window.

'Oh...right,' Ritchie muttered.

'I'm afraid,' Fay explained, moving over to the couch, 'you'll have to sleep here. We've only got two bedrooms. I hope it'll be alright.'

'It's fine.' Right now she wouldn't have minded stretching out on the floor for the night. Anywhere at all would have done, as long as she could be alone. It was a terrible thing to have to admit that after travelling so far to meet her brothers all she really wanted now was some peace and quiet. Even if Fay hadn't been around she would have been afraid to talk to them in case she spoke out of turn. She felt the ground seeming to give way beneath her feet and then slowly lift her as if she were still on board ship. She wondered if her mind too had become unbalanced.

Fay gathered some sheets and blankets from the long press, holding her foot to the boxes which threatened to tumble out once again. As Nora helped her to make up the bed no words passed between them. It seemed like a kind of truce had been secretly agreed. When they'd finished, Fay attached a length of cord to some wall-hooks and hung a sheet along it, dividing off the corner from the rest of the room.

'You can store your clothes in the boys' room,' Fay suggested and they brought her in through yet another door leading off the sitting room.

Here, there was just about enough space for two beds and a wardrobe. A long window, like the one in the front of the apartment, gave a view over the backs of the darkened houses on the street behind.

She was glad to get a chance to be alone with her brothers. There would be no more questions, she decided,s but perhaps she could make up for what had gone on earlier.

'I'm sorry I was so catty,' she told them, 'I feel awful queasy since the boat and it's so...different here...everything...'

Her attempt to ease the tense situation was having the opposite effect. The boys grew even more uncomfortable. She found some space in the wardrobe for her things. From the mirror on the inside of the wardrobe door, she saw Denis and Ritchie looking glumly at each other and she felt heartsick. When she turned to go, Ritchie broke the silence.

'Tomorrow, we'll show you the neighbourhood,' he said, 'after we get back from school.'

'That'll be nice,' she smiled, disguising a sudden panic.

With the boys at school and Phil gone to the bank, she would have to spend the best part of the day with her young aunt. Not only tomorrow but perhaps for weeks.

'When do you get holidays from school?' she asked as calmly as she could.

'Only a week to go,' Denis cried.

Nora was only half-relieved, like a prisoner whose sentence, though reduced, still seems interminably long.

'Goodnight, lads,' she said.

'We're real glad you came,' Ritchie declared. 'We thought we might never see you again.'

Denis nodded in agreement but didn't speak. She was lifted by Ritchie's quiet outburst. It seemed to offer her a second chance, a new start with them. If only they would ask about their father, she thought, then the day might not seem such a disaster after all. Then again the boys had grown but they were still, in many ways, just children. She felt sure that they'd really talk to her and ask about father when they were ready. She would have to prove they could trust her first, she supposed. It had been a bad start but she would gain their confidence yet.

Back in the sitting room Fay was waiting for her. For a moment, Nora was afraid she'd be forced to make more polite conversation. Instead, Fay stifled a rather obvious yawn and stretched lazily.

'I'm heading away to bed,' she said, 'See you in the morning.'

As Nora put on her night clothes, one of the many framed sketches on the sitting room walls caught her eye. It was a familiar scene, the Custom House in Dublin. Though it was a very accurate drawing it was somehow too perfect to be real. At the bottom right hand corner was the unmistakable signature of her uncle and even this had a curious formality about it: 'Philip J. Canavan: 1921'.

Looking around she saw that there were twelve pictures hanging here. All but one depicted well-known Dublin sights. Trinity College, Dublin Castle, The Four Courts where the first shells of the Civil War shattered the uneasy peace of Irish independence. Each one was as precisely drawn as the next.

But, almost hidden away in the alcove above the radio, a very different picture hung. This was of an ordinary street. Was it Clanbrassil Street? It was difficult to be certain because here the buildings were a mere backdrop to the hordes of people going about their business. It was a scene full of life and, Nora decided, it was the presence of ordinary men, women and children that made it so different.

You could almost hear the street noises as you looked at it and each face, down to the smallest child's, expressed something of the uniqueness of every human being. The signature too was different. 'Phil Canavan: '23' it announced, less grandly than before. It was as if he'd tried this new style just once and then given it up. Nora was at a loss to know why. Soon, however, her attention was drawn away from the pictures altogether.

On the bookshelf near the boys' bedroom door stood three glittering trophies and she went quietly to read the inscriptions. They'd all been won by Denis at his school for what was described as the 'Hundred-yard Dash'. Somehow, the presence of these trophies eased her fears about her brother. They seemed to prove that despite her doubts he'd settled well into his new life.

She switched off the light but even with the blinds down the room was filled with the pale glow of the street lamps outside. The window was closed but there was still a muffled roar of passing cars. The couch wasn't altogether uncomfortable but was certainly very narrow and each time she turned, which was often, she did so very carefully.

Long after Fay had finished pottering about in the kitchen, Nora lay wide awake and sweating in the hothouse silence of the apartment. She threw off one and then the second of her blankets. Now even the flimsy sheet covering her weighed like the heaviest eiderdown. Her eyelids refused stubbornly to remain closed over her stinging eyeballs. The traffic bothered her more and more and she couldn't figure out where all these people could be going at such a late hour.

Soon she was aware of voices too from the street, some of them quite child-like or at least those of young people. She drew back the blind a little and saw, at the far end of the street near the strangely out-of-place grey building, a gang of boys scuttling around the corner into a dark alley. She wondered what kind of parent could allow children out into the dangerous city streets at night.

The events of the day crowded in upon her and even in the darkness she blushed to think of how she'd acted these last few hours. If the long sea journey had turned the robust hurlers into children, she mused, it had made a cantankerous old biddy of her. Though she knew she hadn't given Phil and especially Fay a chance, she couldn't quite convince herself that her doubts were totally misplaced.

She drifted into that hazy no-man's land between waking and sleeping. There, where the sounds of reality are transformed by the tired mind to something altogether different, she searched for some valley of quietude. The surge of automobiles became for her the roar of desert winds. Street voices became the conspiratorial whispers of unseen enemies. From the waking distance behind her came an insistent sound like the banging of metal in a forge just over the brow of the hill that was sleep. It seemed important. It seemed to be trying to tell her something.

She followed the dull ringing as it descended into a cool unremembered place, like a bell clanging a warning into eternity.

CHAPTER 8

Nora had planned to stay in bed, pretending to sleep, for as long as possible the following morning to avoid Fay. As it happened, no such pretence was necessary. At two o'clock in the afternoon she was still dozing blissfully. Phil's early departure for work and the boys' bustling off to school had failed to rouse her. When Fay opened the sitting room window just a few inches to freshen the air at around eleven Nora was likewise unmoved. The commerce of traffic and passers-by beneath the window might as well not have existed so deep was her slumber.

When she did wake at last, it was to the sound of pots and pans rattling and echoing. The sunlight warmed her face at first but soon thickened into something more heavy and oppressive. Already she felt the nightdress damp on her back.

The noise from the kitchen stopped and Nora's mind swam away into a state of drowsiness again.

'I hope I didn't wake you,' Fay said cheerfully as she edged back the improvised curtain a little. Not having heard her aunt's footsteps, Nora was startled into wakefulness.

'Did you sleep alright? You look kind of hunched-up in there.'

'I'm fine,' Nora said, realising when she tried to move that her neck was stiff and sore.

'The guys will be back soon. I'm getting some lunch for them. Would you like to eat?'

Nora looked over at the clock on the wall. She couldn't believe she'd slept for so long. It didn't feel that way. Her head was still fuzzy as hell and she didn't feel at all rested.

'I'm sorry I stayed in bed all...'

'Hey, you needed to.'

The sun caught the highlights in her strawberry-blonde hair, her face was a perfect yellowy gold without a trace of powder or paint. Why did she bother to wear make-up at all? Nora was sure her own tired face needed masking more than Fay's ever would.

As soon as Fay left, Nora slipped into her dressing-gown and went to her brothers' room. Sorting through her clothes she realised that nothing she'd brought was suited to this torrid heat. The warmest summers at home paled in comparison to the climate in this urban jungle. Even as she dressed the moisture trickled down her spine. She sat on the bed beside the wardrobe and waited for the boys to return.

As the minutes passed she became more and more conscious of Fay's busy presence around the apartment. She suspected a growing impatience in her aunt's movements and the sudden switching on of the radio to a blaring pitch. She got to her feet and steeled herself to go out to the kitchen and offer, by way of a peace gesture, to lend a hand.

Just then, that mysterious bell-like clanging she'd dreamt of the night before intruded, faintly but quite clearly, on her troubled thoughts. For some mysterious reason she felt the sound was a warning. She went and opened the door, certain that the tidal wave of music from the radio would banish her unease.

For the briefest of instants, she thought that the insistent ringing came from somewhere behind her, beyond the window in the boys' room. Suddenly Ritchie's voice came booming up the stairs. She was so happy to hear him that she almost laughed aloud at her foolish imaginings. Somehow, when she greeted them on the landing this time, the meeting was infinitely better than at the pier. There was none of the desperate searching for words of the previous day. And Denis had a gift wrapped in silver paper for her.

'You shouldn't be throwing away your money,' she blurted out.

'We went fifty-fifty,' he explained proudly, 'me and Ritchie.'

It was a pearl necklace. Not a real one but no less welcome for that. She held it between her palms. It felt as cool as the pebbles from the bed of a stream.

'Why don't you try it on,' Ritchie demanded.

She placed the necklace around her neck and he fumbled with the catch until Denis intervened.

'You can't do it, 'cause you bite your nails.'

'No I don't.'

'Sure you do.'

They argued and caffled but it was all in fun. They went inside to the kitchen where Fay was taking a pot from the cooker.

'See what we bought Nora,' Ritchie exclaimed.

'Hey, I'm jealous. Look at them *poils*.'

They ate quickly and talked freely. Soon, they were stepping down on to the street outside. If it was hot in the apartment, out here it was positively sweltering. They crossed immediately to the shade on the other side. Walking along towards the grey-columned building up ahead they explained its significance.

Like many of the streets here this one didn't have any official name, only a number. It was an idea that suited everyone except those who lived there. Not many people like to live on a street with no name. There is something inhuman about it. So, all of the streets in the locality had nicknames and that was where that misplaced structure came in. It was once a bathhouse, used by the locals before bathrooms became more common in the apartment houses. In previous times the grey building had been called 'the wash-basin'. Now it was empty and disused but the street itself had become known as 'Wash-Basin Street'.

This explained the strange name above the grocery store she'd noticed when the cab had brought her to the street the day before. It was to this very shop that they were now going. Fay had given the boys some money to buy sweets or 'candy' as she'd put it.

When they reached the shop Nora was surprised to see, in smaller lettering below the main sign, the words, 'Proprietor, W.D. Ryan'. Back in Tipperary there were so many Ryans that, like these numbered streets, each family had a nickname. Some of these nicknames were unusual, like Ryan Kites. Others were downright insulting, for example, Ryan Cribbers.

Ritchie told her that this particular family was second-generation Irish. The aging grandmother who sat all day in the shop was from the Silvermines, a small village in north Tipperary. He'd told the old woman of Nora's impending visit and she'd asked him to bring his sister to see her.

'I'll wait here,' Denis said, screwing up his dark eyebrows as he stood against the wall beside the shop window.

It seemed to Nora that he was trying very hard to hide himself from the view of those inside. In their Dublin days, Denis was always first in line when there was money to be spent on sweets. Now, he looked pale and agitated and was quickly losing patience with Ritchie who was searching through his pockets for the nickels and dimes.

'Hurry it up, will you,' he urged.

'What's wrong, Denis?' Nora asked.

'Nothing,' came the sharp reply and then fumbling about for an explanation, he added, 'The old lady, see, she goes on like I'm a two-year-old, tossing my hair and pinching my cheeks. It drives me up the wall.'

Nora remained unconvinced. He was too jumpy by half.

'She thinks I'm cute,' Denis muttered half-heartedly.

The old woman dabbed tears from her eyes with her twisted, arthritic hands when she was introduced to Nora. Her grey hair, swept tightly back into a bun, and the stiff collar of her black dress gave no impression of severity. Her small face was kind and open. Though she seemed quite tiny in the high-ceilinged shop, Nora could almost feel the strength of the old woman's determination. The kind of determination that helps people survive against all the odds.

'Every day of my life, I miss Tipperary,' old Mrs Ryan began, 'but there's not a day passes that I'm not glad I came here with Bill, God rest his soul. We'd have none of this back home, no matter how hard we tried.'

Nora wished she could talk more freely to the old woman who was so anxious to hear how her country was settling down after the Civil War. But her mind was with Denis, as he waited outside in an inexplicable state of anxiety.

'Not that we ever had it easy here either, mind you,' Mrs Ryan went on. 'By God, it was tough in the early days and we have our troubles now too. I wish to God they were all decent people around here like the Canavans. Feck the hairs off your eyebrows in these parts when you weren't looking. God forgive me for swearing. Only two weeks ago we were robbed for the umpteenth time.'

What kind of neighbourhood was this to live in, Nora thought? Surely Phil could find an apartment somewhere else? Perhaps it wasn't such a bad thing after all they were going to have to leave the apartment. The sooner the better, was Nora's verdict.

'But here,' the old woman continued since no one else was talking, 'there's no point in complaining. D'ye know I've a grandson out in Chicago and he's a medical doctor. Doctor Timothy Ryan. I never thought I'd see the day. Makes it all worthwhile, seeing your own do so well.'

Somehow, the old woman reminded Nora of Molly. They seemed to share the same toughness behind a frail exterior. As Mrs Ryan talked on, Nora wondered if Molly was at this very moment down in that hospital in Cork and already over her operation and waiting to have the bandages removed from her eyes. Or perhaps she was on her way home having been told that there was no hope of regaining her sight. She felt ashamed to have given so little thought to her aunt this past week. For some reason this sense of shame made her even more angry with Denis for not coming in to see Mrs Ryan.

As they left, the old woman called after them, 'Bring young Dinny with you next time. I haven't seen him in ages. I think he's out with me.'

Back on the street they saw that Denis had already moved on ahead. When they caught up with him and came to share out the sweets, Nora found she had no appetite for them.

'She's a nice woman,' she told Denis, 'I don't know why you didn't have the common decency to go in and talk to her.'

'She thinks the sun shines out of Denis' back...'

'Ritchie,' she snapped, 'Mind your tongue.'

'Young Dinny,' Ritchie jeered, copying the old woman's tremulous voice.

Nora had to stand between them as first Denis and then Ritchie lashed out with flailing fists. She was horrified at the scene they were creating in front of all the passersby.

'You're making a show of us,' she whispered loudly.

Denis pulled himself away from her and backed off. The cynical twist of his mouth cut her to the quick. He looked like a wild cat ready to pounce.

'D'ye really think anyone notices,' he snarled, 'Nobody gives a goddam.'

He stormed off along the pavement not even bothering to step aside for the young woman who approached with a small child in tow.

'Watch where you're goin', dummy!' she yelled.

'Aw, shut your trap, lady,' Denis roared and broke into a run, not stopping until he was out of sight.

The child at the woman's side started wailing and she whacked it across the ear, calling out, 'You wanna turn out like that little bum?'

Ritchie stood open-mouthed as he stared in the direction his brother had fled. The bag of sweets had fallen from his hands but he didn't bother picking them up.

'I'll buy you some more,' Nora told him.

'Don't matter,' he said.

'Tell me the truth,' she asked, 'Is he always like this or is it something to do with me?'

'Naw, it ain't you,' he assured her, 'He don't even treat me like a brother no more.'

'So, when did all this start?'

'I don't know. Months, maybe.'

She was convinced he knew more than he was pretending. True, she hadn't been with him for two years but there are things you don't forget. Like the tricks that people who are close to you get up to when they're hiding secrets. Sometimes you get it wrong but most of the time you have a fair idea when they're being less than honest with you. Often, it is something as innocent as the way Ritchie tugged at the sleeve of his shirt, as he did now.

'If Denis is in trouble you should tell me, and maybe I could help him.'

'It's nothing like that,' Ritchie mumbled, ''Cept maybe it's the guys he hangs around with.'

'Who are these guys?' It felt strange to Nora to be slipping into this American slang.

'Just a bunch of guys...round here, you know,' he muttered, pulling at his sleeve again. 'They're kinda wild.'

'Wild? What's that supposed to mean?'

Ritchie began to walk back towards the apartment house. She held back from grabbing his arm and instead walked along beside him, staying outwardly calm. If she was going to get anything out of him, the best way was to do it gently.

'Denis was always a bit on the mad side, wasn't he?' she joked.

'I suppose.'

He refused to say any more so there was nothing she could do but remain patient. Even if it took days she was sure he would eventually tell what was bottled up inside him. But the days passed and as she lay on her makeshift bed four nights later she was still no nearer the truth.

Denis had apologised for acting so badly and seemed to make a greater effort to be pleasant to her and even to Ritchie. However, those times when she looked at him without his noticing he appeared glum and withdrawn. She had, too, become a little more comfortable with Fay. The secret with her it seemed was never to be surprised at what she did or said. And if you were, not to let it show. As for Phil, despite his constant good humour, he grew more and more tired looking from one day to the next. Now, when he nodded off in his favourite chair by the radio, it was a chilling reminder of how her father looked in the bad days in Inchicore. Though he didn't drink at all, he seemed more worn down than the worst alcoholic.

After that first night of rest Nora had slipped back into the pattern of broken sleep that had begun on board the SS *Bremen*. And this night was no different. The muggy heat had become, if anything, even more unbearable. Phil told her how the locals called these the 'dog days', and the description was fitting. The smallest effort brought out streams of sweat. All you could do was lie in the shade like the dogs did. For Nora this meant long hours in the apartment so that already, after only four days, she felt as much a prisoner as she had on the ship.

If the daylight hours were long, the nights were interminable. Her fitful sleep was constantly bothered by the same unmusical metallic noises that returned without fail as soon as darkness fell. Even now, as she waited for yet another wave of sleep to come, the tuneless vibrations rang in her ears again.

She sat up wearily, gasping for breath and pressed her palms to her ears to drown away the tormenting sound. Silence descended and a wisp of air from the open window touched her cheek. She suddenly felt wide awake and a shiver went through her like a memory of cold.

From the far side of the apartment, beyond the sitting room, beyond the boys' room came a very real banging. All at once she knew that the faint clatter hadn't come from her dreams. It was as clear and distinct now as the hurried beating of her heart. She threw on her dressing-gown and inched across the sitting room noiselessly. Already the clanging noise was fading but she was still surprised that no one else seemed to have been disturbed by it.

Easing open the door of her brothers' room she peered into the semi-darkness at the far window. Suddenly her attention was drawn to Denis' bed. The sheets were drawn back and it was quite empty. Ritchie was fast asleep in his own bed but she switched on the light anyway. She had to be sure but there could be no doubt about it now.

Denis was gone.

CHAPTER 9

Ritchie squinted and floundered about fearfully in the bright light. Nora was in such a panic that she felt no pity for him. She shook him so violently that his confusion turned to stubborn anger.

'Where is he?'

'What'ye talking about?' he groaned, 'What'ye go waking me up for!'

'You must have heard him going,' she insisted.

Ritchie hadn't yet looked around the room. His face was buried in the pillow now as if in search of the sleep that had been stolen from him. He moaned softly and curled into a ball beneath the linen sheet.

'It's Denis,' she said, tugging at him, 'He's not in his bed.'

The tousled head of fair hair emerged slowly. His heavy-lidded eyes were glazed over. When he spoke it was with a hint of exasperation.

'Did you try the bathroom, by any chance?'

'I'm sure I'd have heard him go out there,' she said but she went and checked anyway.

He wasn't there. She looked into the kitchen quietly so as not to waken Fay. In the shaft of light from the boys' room she could see the clock on the sitting room wall. Quarter past one. Phil would be back from the warehouse in less than an hour. She couldn't figure out how Denis could have left the

apartment without her noticing. She knew how lightly she
was sleeping these nights, the smallest sound waking her. He
would have had to pass through the sitting room where she
slept. Or was there some other way?

Back in her brothers' room she went to the window. Ritchie
watched her apprehensively. Looking out into the night from
the brightly-lit room, she could see nothing but her own reflection. She went and switched off the light. Soon the outline of
buildings came into view, rimmed with haze from the city
lights. Windows took shape in the apartment houses behind.
Then she noticed a curious criss-cross shape from the bottom to
the top of each house. By and by it became clearer. It was an
outside stairway and if she wasn't mistaken, a metal one.

She opened the window and as she'd guessed a similar
stairway was attached to the back wall of this house too. She
stepped out on to the landing and the metal rang out softly
beneath her bare feet. It was the same sound that had been
troubling her since her first night here.

The low hum of the city reached her but nearby there was
only silence. There was no knowing where Denis had disappeared to but it was clear this wasn't the first time he'd gone
out late at night. She climbed back inside and sat on Denis'
bed. Ritchie was lying back on the pillow, glad of the dark.

'Are you going to tell me what this is all about?' she asked
quietly.

'I swear to God, I don't know. It never happened before.'

'Don't lie to me, Ritchie.'

'I...I...' he mumbled, 'He'll tell you himself if he wants to.'

Somehow the sticky air didn't bother her now. She felt the
same windswept chill she'd experienced on the deck of the
SS *Bremen*. Now, however, the wind came from the torrent of
loneliness inside her; the cold, from her brother's words.

'You're afraid of him, aren't you,' she said cruelly, 'Afraid
of your own brother.'

'No, he's the one who's afraid.'

'Of who?' she demanded.

He went quiet again. Nora decided to wait as long as it took for Denis to return. She closed out the door so that Phil wouldn't notice anything amiss when he got back from work. A vague fear stirred in her that he'd look in on the boys before going to bed but it was a chance she'd have to take. The wait was shorter than she'd expected.

Denis was almost at the window when she heard his footsteps. He hauled himself inside and moved towards his bed. Nora held her breath and the flood of anger that would certainly be released with it. Her hand found his wrist and she gripped it with all the strength she could muster.

'Where were you?' she shouted.

'Nora, you frightened the life out of me.'

Her fingernails dug into his skin. She knew she was hurting him but she didn't care.

'What about me!' she exclaimed, 'Do you not think I've been worried sick here waiting for you?'

'Let go!' he cried, 'You're breaking my wrist.'

'It's no more than you deserve, you pup. Where were you?'

'Mind your own business.'

'I'm your sister, so it *is* my business.'

He dragged his hand away from her roughly.

'Some sister,' he seethed.

Her first instinct was to wallop him but her anger was giving way to a pain that cut through to her very soul. *His* anger, however, grew with every word he spat out.

'Some sister,' he repeated, 'Left us high and dry. Didn't even bother to say goodbye. You're worse than the old man, that lousy drunken slob. Yeah, but you're all pally-wally with him now, ain't you.'

He was crying tears that had been welling up inside for two years. Ritchie too was sobbing into his pillow. All the good things that had happened to Nora since she'd gone to Tipperary faded into nothingness. Here they were, she thought in her desperation, the broken down ruins of a family. Each one of them alone and empty like those tumbled castles in their solitary fields scattered along the length and breadth of Ireland. Sad and bitter memories were all they had in common now.

Down below, the front door of the apartment house banged shut. Phil was home. She stood up slowly and steadying herself found her way to the door.

'I'm sorry you feel like that,' she said.

As she closed the door behind her she heard him whisper, 'I don't feel nothin', I don't wanna feel nothin'.'

She hadn't yet got behind the curtain around her bed when Phil opened the sitting room door.

'You alright, Nora?'

'Fine.... I thought I heard a noise on that stairs behind the house.'

Why she let this much slip she couldn't understand. She had intended to say something about going to the bathroom. He seemed to hesitate but perhaps she only imagined he did.

'Ah, the fire escape,' he laughed.

That was probably the reason for his hesitation, she thought. He had obviously been trying to figure out what she'd meant by 'a stairs behind the house'.

'Don't worry about that,' he assured her, 'It's probably some kids messing around.'

'At this hour?'

She sensed his hesitation again.

'We got some wild ones in those apartments out back.'

We've got some wild ones here too, she almost blurted out. Then again, he was too busy with his two jobs to notice what was going on right under his nose. For now, there could be no question of telling him. That would only deepen the bad feeling between herself and Denis. This was a family matter and, as far as she was concerned now, Phil and Fay were not 'family'. If Denis was going off the rails because of his bitterness towards her father and herself then it was up to her to make him trust in her again.

Nora was willing to admit that Phil and Fay weren't to blame for his waywardness. As Molly often said when things went wrong and people were seeking to lay the blame, 'It doesn't have to be anyone's fault.' The plain fact was they had taken on too much responsibility. It wasn't possible to work so much and take care of a family too. Not in New York.

As she thought about her plan of action it came to her that not having told Phil could prove to be the turning point in winning Denis over. If Phil really was unaware of Denis' escapades, and for the moment she was inclined to believe this was so, then she had spared her brother from immediate punishment. Now, Denis would more than likely figure that she'd take every opportunity to blackmail him into giving up these night time pranks. Instead, she would lull him into a false sense of security by pretending that nothing had happened tonight. Knowing him as well as she imagined she did she thought he would lie low for a while and then take to the streets again. Her plan was to wait for this to happen, follow him and confront these fellows he was mixing with.

But her calculations were shattered even as she tried to imagine what that confrontation would be like. The fire escape steps rang out their discordant, descending scales again.

When she reached her brothers' room, Ritchie was standing by the window.

'I tried to stop him,' he said, 'but he wouldn't listen.'

'I'm going after him,' Nora announced, even though it was clear Denis had too great a headstart on her.

'If I knew where they hang out, I'd tell you,' Ritchie said, 'I swear to God, I would, Nora.'

She slipped on a dress over her nightclothes and threw on the first pair of shoes that came to hand in the darkened bedroom.

'You can't go out there on your own,' Ritchie cried. 'I'll get dressed too.'

'There isn't time,' she hissed, climbing out on to the fire escape. 'I want you to wait here and if I'm not back in an hour you'll have to tell Phil.'

'Try the bathhouse,' Ritchie said wearily, 'but don't tell him I told you.'

The descent was painfully slow, her every step seeming to clamour out into the night. Every muscle in her body was unbearably cramped. The bulky nightgown, clamped to her skin by the close-fitting dress, made an ordeal of each movement of her arms. Her shoes were inexplicably tight and pinched her heels.

Down in the alleyway behind the house, the dark shadows seemed to contain unspeakable dangers. There was just light enough to see that to her right was a dead end. She moved quickly to her left and at the corner found only another alleyway. She could have turned in either direction but something told her to head left again.

There were two further turns into widening alleyways before she found herself on Wash-Basin Street. A car with its headlights switched off turned into the street and she ducked into the shadows until it had gone from sight. The coast clear, she headed for the lane beside the once-stately building.

When she reached the place she looked down the dark passage but could see no light of any kind. The sound of her own heartbeat echoed like savage drums. Then she heard voices. By now her fear had been replaced by indignation. She stepped into the gloomy depths of the alleyway.

It was so narrow that she could touch the walls on either side as she went along. The voices became more and more clear until she came to a heavy door. She could just about make out its high, arched shape and the ornate outline of a massive door handle. For all its bulk, it opened noiselessly.

Before her was a stairwell and as she inched upwards she was intrigued by the curious quality of the light here. It wasn't sharp like that light from the electric bulbs in the apartment but more like the softer glow of the street lamps. There were four, perhaps five distinct voices, none of them recognisable.

When she reached the top of the stairs she saw why the light in here was so different. The ceiling overhead was composed entirely of coloured glass that bore the kinds of figures you would expect only in a church window. Angels with harps and bearded men in robes. The effect was almost magical, the dull yellow glow from the street transformed to reds and greens and blues. This, however, was no time for magic. The prospect of what lay ahead was too real.

The first thing that hit her as she pushed open yet another heavily-ornamented door, was the stinging haze of cigarette smoke. Eight young faces met her astonished gaze. Some, including Denis, were visibly frightened. Others simply looked once and turned their attention to the card game they were playing. One face stared back at her defiantly. She was so taken aback by the fellow that the scene behind him took some time to sink in.

He was short, no more than a few inches taller than Denis, though he was certainly older. Sixteen or seventeen, she guessed. What was extraordinary about him was that he was dressed, unlike all the others, in the kind of suit and hat only an adult would wear. In fact, in New York, only a certain type of man would wear them. The shady type.

The suit, cut to perfection, was a black pinstripe. The hat pulled down over his forehead was black too. His black shirt was set off with a white tie and his shoes were two-toned, black and white. From his lips a cigarette dangled. He was a perfect miniature of the kind of screen gangster Nora was familiar with from the Stella Cinema.

'Welcome to the Foggy Club, honey,' he announced, the cigarette still in his mouth.

She might have laughed at this absurd little fellow but at that moment, Denis exhaled for the first time since she'd walked in. His breath was a cloud of smoke.

'Denis,' she called, 'You're coming with me.'

The boy pretending to be a man turned to Denis.

'So, who's the dame, kid?' he asked with a leer.

Denis looked away towards the enormous, empty pool in the centre of the place. When he looked back it was to fix Nora with an evil glare.

'She's my sister.'

'You never told me you had such a sweet-looking sister,' the fellow said, grinning widely at Nora. 'De name's Feeney. Danny Feeney and dese guys is de "Weebies".'

He moved a step closer and she drew herself up to her full height. The top of his head was about level with her chin.

'Get out of my way, you little scut,' she warned.

'Listen, lady, you're talking to Danny Feeney and...'

'I don't care if I'm talking to the Archbishop of New York!' she yelled, 'I'm taking my brother out of this rat hole.'

She tried to bustle past him but he stood his ground. He raised his cigarette from his mouth and moved it towards her face. Nora swung her fist but he caught it without even looking and held it in a vice-like grip. The pain was excruciating and though she tried to conceal it, her whole body was shaking. His unflinching eyes were cold and hard.

'Show a little respect, sis,' he warned and called over his shoulder to Denis, 'You wanna go home and have your big sister sing you a lullaby?'

Denis was hiding behind some of the others now so that

she wouldn't see him. Or perhaps because he didn't want to see what happening to her.

'I ain't goin' nowhere,' he muttered.

'Can't hear you,' Feeney bawled, tightening his hold on Nora's arm.

'I said, I ain't goin' nowhere.'

'You heard what he said, sweetie. Now clear outa here.'

He pushed her against the wall. It was humiliating to be pushed around by such a weed of a fellow but Nora was helpless. No matter how she struggled, kicking her legs back or driving her free elbow into his stomach, she couldn't break free. He seemed to possess a strength far beyond his years or his small stature.

'I'm gonna let you go now, sis,' he whispered in her ear, 'and I want you to walk outa here and forget what you seen, OK?'

Nora refused to answer. He twisted her arm until it seemed it would spring from its socket. She pressed her forehead to the wall in a spasm of pain but she wasn't giving in. She felt his grip loosen and with one last effort she swung around. He had anticipated her move and stepped back quickly. Her flailing arm swung at fresh air. She tried again but he ducked cooly and grinned at her.

'You're some tough cookie, honey,' he said, exhaling another draught of smoke into her face.

'And you're a little pig.'

He straightened his hat and fixed his silly white tie. He couldn't quite figure out how to handle Nora. Nobody came back looking for more once they'd suffered the venom of his attacks. Not until now.

'Denis,' he shouted, careful not to take his eyes off her, 'Take de lady home.'

Denis emerged shamefaced from the group gathered behind Danny Feeney. As bitter as she felt towards the young thug in the suit, it was nothing compared to what she felt about her brother. He had stood by as she was mistreated without so much as a whimper of protest. She met his pleading eyes with an icy glare.

'Hey, I like de shoes,' Danny chuckled as she and Denis backed away to the door.

He was pointing at Nora's feet and the gang behind him were cackling like a flock of geese. She was white with fury. She stared into his small eyes and his smile took on a nervous tremor. The shoes belonged to Denis.

'And I love your suit,' she retorted. 'Where did you get it? From a circus midget?'

'Scram, honey,' he rasped, 'before I change my mind.'

Behind him one of the gang giggled and he belted him across the head. It was time to leave.

All along Wash-Basin Street, Denis tried to keep up with her. Over and over, he repeated his weak words of apology. She said nothing until they reached the foot of the fire escape leading to the apartment. There, she got behind him, blocking off any chance of escape.

'Get up there fast,' she said, 'It's time Phil heard about your antics.'

CHAPTER 10

They stood around the table in the centre of the sitting room, Phil and Fay at one end, Nora at the other. Between them, Denis leaned against the side, his eyes averted. Ritchie was in his room humming quietly to himself to drown the angry voices.

Nora was explaining how she'd followed Denis and what she'd discovered. Her feelings about Phil and Fay spilled out and she held nothing back.

They were too preoccupied with making money to bother about the boys, she claimed. Too soft on them too and behaving more like irresponsible brother and sister than parents. Had they no idea how a mother or father should act? How could they not see what was going on?

Fay tried to object and Denis made some weak protests. Each time, Phil told them to hear Nora out. His air of calm annoyed Nora even more. His head nodded as if in agreement with everything she said, and waited patiently for her attack to end. She had expected, had wanted a real argument. She wanted him to offer excuses. There was no satisfaction in attacking someone who appeared so unwilling to defend himself. She banged her fist on the table in her frustration.

'For God's sake, say something,' she shouted finally.

Phil pulled back a chair from the table and sat down wearily.

'Denis, go to bed now,' he said quietly and turned to his wife. 'Best get some shut-eye, honey.'

Fay stared at Nora. Her face was filled not with hate but with hurt. She seemed younger, more girlish than ever without her make-up. Nora was too irate to feel sorry for her. She rounded on her uncle.

'Aren't you going to punish him?' she asked in disbelief. 'He was *smoking* over there.'

'I'll talk to Denis in the morning.'

Denis walked away towards his room. At the door he swivelled around and yelled at Nora.

'Why don't you go back where you belong and mind your own business!'

'Denis,' Fay cried and hustled him into his room.

The minutes ticked away on the clock as she and Phil listened to the muffled sounds from inside. Eventually, Fay emerged and without so much as a glance at Nora went away to her own room. The silence continued for a little while until Phil stood up and came to sit beside Nora.

'I'm not sure where to start,' he said, staring at his outstretched fingers.

'You could try telling the truth. You knew Denis was up to no good.'

'It's not so easy, Nora. The whole thing is very...very complicated.'

'Complicated? It's dead simple, if you can't be honest...' she said making as if to leave the table.

'Nora,' he pleaded, holding her arm lightly, 'hear me out, will you.'

She sidled away from his touch and with a challenging glare waited for his explanation.

'When we got your mother's letter two years back we had to make some hard choices and OK, we made them. But it wasn't just as simple as that. We lived in a one-bedroomed apartment and when I say one room, I mean one room. Eat, sleep, the lot, in one room. Not because we wanted it that way but it was all we could afford.'

Nora tried to ease herself from her chair. He spoke with such passion that she could feel droplets of his spittle on her face. She was horrified at what she'd begun.

'Sit down and listen,' he demanded. 'So, we got ourselves a bigger place here, right? And to do that we borrowed money and we've been working our tails off ever since paying back that loan. You think I wouldn't prefer to sit down at night and read or listen to my radio? Or that Fay actually enjoys spending her evenings down on Broadway working for mug's money? I don't like saying this but it seems to me you came here hoping you'd find trouble, Nora, because deep down you don't want the boys to be happy here.'

'That's not true,' she objected, but it felt like a slap in the face, the kind that brings you back to your senses.

'You just think about it.'

'None of that has anything to do with what happened tonight,' she said evenly though her heart was racing. 'Denis was out with a gang of thugs and I know it's not the first time.'

Phil strode away to the sitting room window. He looked out into the night like he was searching for something. He drew in a deep breath and faced her again.

'OK, I knew something was up,' he admitted, raising his hand to stop her interrupting, 'and I did try to stop it but...well, it didn't work out. For the moment, my hands are tied, I can't do anything about it just yet.'

'You can't do anything about it?'

'No, I can't,' he insisted. 'These are dangerous people. I don't mean the kids he's hanging around with but...certain other people. A lot of stuff is going on here that I can't tell you about. There are problems. But everything will be sorted out in a matter of weeks, I promise.'

Nora remembered his reaction when he'd heard she was staying longer than he'd thought.

'That's why you didn't want me around too long.'

'Nora, I wish things could be better here. For your sake, for all our sakes but...'

'And these dangerous people, whoever they are, can't you go to the police about them?'

He shook his head and smiled wistfully.

'There's nothing to worry about,' he reassured her, 'I'm going to let you in on a little secret. Fay knows but the boys don't.'

She wasn't sure if she wanted to know any more but she listened anyway.

'We're going to be moving out to the Midwest, to a small town south of Chicago called Dennsville, all four of us,' he whispered. 'Away from the city where the boys can have a decent life. There's lots of good people here but you get mixed up with the few bad apples and it's a living hell.'

'What's stopping you from going now?' she asked.

'Like I said, there's some sorting out to be done first.'

It seemed to Nora that Phil had talked a lot and in the end told her nothing that mattered. His words enveloped her like a fog. Dangerous people, things to be sorted out, a loan he was trying to pay off, a move to some place unknown to her. Her head throbbed in a daze of tiredness.

'You'll just have to trust me,' he said. 'Get some sleep if you can.'

As she found her way behind the curtain to her couch she heard him call softly.

'I'm sorry your visit's been such a mess, I really am.'

The days and weeks loomed ahead like an eternity. There was nothing worse than having to linger where you weren't wanted. But what choice was there? There was no escape and none either from Phil's accusation: *You don't want the boys to be happy.* The idea, at first preposterous, slowly began to seep into her brain until she could think of nothing else. Its meaning soon became all too clear.

If the boys could be happy thousands of miles away without having seen her for two years then, in a real sense, Nora didn't matter to them. All this time she'd held on to the certainty that she was their one, irreplaceable sister, that they still needed her. Perhaps it was true that when she'd come to New York she had to find some way to confirm that she was still needed. She had found plenty such reasons but it seemed that the last person the boys would accept help from was their sister.

A few hours later when the city had swapped its night glow for a deep-red dawn, Nora felt nothing but regret. If only she had slept better since she'd come to New York she might never have heard Denis' footsteps on the fire escape. If she hadn't taken an instant dislike to Fay and harboured such suspicions about Phil, they might have got along. If she hadn't tried so hard to do what she thought was her sisterly duty then Denis would never had said such cruel and unforgivable things to her. But the final regret was the worst. If she hadn't come to New York in the first place she would never have had to go through all this misery.

The morning, despite its brightness, seemed to promise only further gloom. From the time Phil left for work until the boys struggled out to school, she longed for silence to descend again on the apartment. She had no wish to talk to anyone, not even Ritchie. There was nothing left for her to say and nothing she wanted to hear from any of them. When the boys left she felt a guilty sense of relief. She had come so far to meet them and now all she wanted to do was avoid them. Her relief, however, was short-lived.

The apartment door opened again and she heard Ritchie calling her name excitedly. He ducked in by the curtain to the side of her couch. In his hand he held a letter.

'The mailman just gave me this. It's for you.'

It was, she thought, more than likely from Peter or one of her friends. She was almost afraid to take it, sure it would only deepen her painful longing for home. Not least because it seemed to her that when she left for home next month she would have lost her brothers forever. She had caused so much trouble now they would never want to see her again. Not even Ritchie's grinning face could convince her otherwise. He left the letter beside her. She couldn't look at it.

'I gotta run,' he said but before he went beyond the curtain, added mysteriously, 'Who do you know in New York?'

'What?' she muttered and sat up with a start.

'See you later, we got a half-day, be back at lunch-hour,' Ritchie called and thundered out of the sitting room and down the stairs.

The letter was indeed date-stamped in New York. Her name and address at the apartment house were neatly typed across its front but for the letter 'a' which was only half-formed. With great trepidation she opened it at last and brought herself to read its contents.

Emblazoned across the top of the single sheet were the words, 'The LaFonde Musical Foundation; Est. 1869.'

As she read on her puzzlement soon gave way to a dizzy mixture of elation and misgiving.

Dear Miss Canavan, the letter began, *I have been requested to consider your candidacy for a place at this Foundation. In this respect, I would suggest that you contact me as soon as possible in order to arrange an audition. I am compelled to inform you that our standards are of the highest order and no favour is shown to any candidate. Musical ability is our sole criterion.*

The signature below was indecipherable, penned with an arrogant flourish. What was abundantly clear though was the identity of the person who had 'requested' the audition. It must certainly have been the stranger from the SS *Bremen*.

Perhaps it was because she'd sunk so deep into despair during the long, eventful night that she now felt so exhilarated. For a while, she could set aside her fear of the stranger and imagine the possibilities opening out before her. At home, she would have to wait another year for an opportunity like this. Even then, what would happen if she failed to get the Waldworth Scholarship? Surely she couldn't expect Peter and Molly to pay her way, as the stranger had offered to? And if she did fail to get the scholarship would she live to regret passing up this chance at the LaFonde Foundation?

Slowly but surely, reality intruded, like the fearful, many-headed monster it often proved to be.

Where would she live while she studied at the Foundation? Surely not with Phil, not after all that had happened? In any case, he was moving the family out of New York. And what of the stranger, what of his terrifying temper, his barely-concealed violent nature? And Molly? How could she desert her when she needed her most? And then came the realisation that she was putting the cart before the horse in all these speculations. The chances were she wouldn't even get past the audition. The writer of this letter was obviously not one who was easily pleased.

In the apartment the day's stagnant heat was beginning to thicken and she felt she must get outside. During her first days in this city she'd vowed never to go out alone. Now fear gave way to desperation. At the kitchen table, Fay was in her nightdress drinking coffee and reading a newspaper. She barely acknowledged Nora's greeting but went and made some breakfast for her. Nora felt like she was bound and gagged. She wanted to run, shout, do anything that would help clear her mind.

When she'd finished eating she got up to leave. Fay looked at her waiting for her to speak. Nora thought she probably expected her to reveal what was in the letter. It was an ideal opportunity, she knew, to take the sting from her attack of the night before, but Nora let it pass.

'Do you mind if I go out for a while?' she asked sweetly.

'Just stick to Wash-Basin Street, alright?' Fay said and Nora detected in her voice a kind of plea, a suggestion that perhaps she give her aunt a second chance to prove herself.

'I'll just go down to see Mrs Ryan in the corner shop. She asked me to call some time.'

'Fine,' Fay sighed, 'only stick to the street, OK?'

Nora descended the rickety stairs and banged out the apartment house door. There was no cooling breeze to greet her, only a wall of solid heat. It didn't matter. She was free for an hour or two from the confines of the small, unwelcoming apartment.

Though in no particular hurry she walked quickly towards Ryan's shop. At the back of her mind was a vague notion that she might seek the old woman's advice on what to do about the Foundation. Mrs Ryan seemed to her the closest she could get to Molly, who would certainly have known what to tell her.

Suddenly, a few paces ahead of her she saw a familiar figure, short and still dressed in his black suit despite the heat. She stopped in her tracks but he'd already spun around as if he'd sensed her presence.

'How you was, honey,' Danny Feeney sneered, blocking her way.

'Let me pass, you little twerp.'

He looked around to see if anyone had heard her and gave her a vicious look.

'I think we should talk,' he said, but it was more a threat than a suggestion. 'Maybe get some things straight.'

'There's nothing to get straight,' she told him, taking courage from the fact that there were lots of people passing by.

'You're leading Denis astray and you're not going to get away with it.'

It suddenly occurred to her that even if Phil wasn't willing to go to the police, there was nothing to stop her doing so.

'I'm going this minute to the police station and telling them about your "Foggy Club".'

He stood aside and swept his hands in the direction she was headed to.

'Go ahead, be my guest, sweetheart,' he chuckled, 'but before you do let me tell you something for nothing. Your little Denis ain't no sweet innocent.'

'What do you mean?'

'Like I said, maybe we should talk. Maybe I can convince you the station house ain't such a good idea. Follow me.' He winked and headed down Wash-Basin Street.

'We can talk right here,' Nora insisted.

'I don't do business on the street, honey,' he told her. 'We'll go sit somewhere. The drinks are on me.'

'I don't drink.'

'We're talking soda pop here,' he laughed. 'Ain't you never heard of Prohibition?'

Cocking his little head, he flashed her what he imagined was a charming smile. He looked to her like a Pekinese begging a dog biscuit.

'You and me,' he said, 'we could be real good friends, you know. You're just my type.'

Nora was astounded. The little weed had clearly taken a fancy to her but his wheedling ways revolted her even more than the roughness she'd experienced at the bathhouse.

'I doubt it,' she said flatly. 'And I'm not going in to some dirty dive with you if that's what you're thinking.'

'I'm taking you to a diner is all. So pipe down, sweetheart.'

Every so often he slowed up a little so she could walk beside him but she wasn't having any of that. She drifted back a step or two each time, not wanting anyone to think she was with him. He strutted along like a peacock, checking himself out in every shop window they passed. More than once he called out to some equally rakish young thugs with a breezy shrug of the shoulders, 'Catch you later. Got myself dated up.'

If this meant what Nora thought it did she wasn't going to let it pass.

'Listen here,' she objected when he repeated it for the third time, 'I don't want you giving the wrong impression about me.'

'Joke, honey. Don't you ever smile?'

'Every time I look at you.'

He stopped dead and looked up at her maliciously.

'If you don't button those pretty lips of yours, I'll snitch on Denis myself. Some of my old man's best friends is cops.'

Five minutes later they were sitting in a diner off Willis Ave, a place filled with couples and young families, the parents trying to control impossible children. Danny carried over two orange-flavoured fizzy drinks the likes of which Nora had never tasted before. The unfamiliar concoction was too sweet by far.

'Great stuff for hangovers but I prefer gin myself,' he boasted. 'Listen, you and me, we got off to a pretty rotten start but...'

'I want to hear about Denis, not about you and me.'

'Yeah, poor little Denis,' he sniggered, opening the buttons of his jacket and spreading himself back lazily on his seat.

'Just tell me,' Nora said angrily, 'and stop prancing around like a prize hen.'

'A prize hen,' he grinned, 'I love it, you look so sweet when you get angry.'

The glass in Nora's hand shook, the sickly-sweet liquid splashing out on to the table.

'Steady up,' he said. 'Alright, I'll tell you about your

brother. He's...how can I put this...he's a valuable member of my gang. D'ye ever see that guy run? He's a "Weebee". See, my gang's called the "Weebees". Great name, ain't it?'

Nora looked suitably unimpressed but he went on regardless.

'The "Weebees". Wash-Basin, you see. W for Wash, B for Basin. So, you get the "Weebees".'

'Did you think that up all by yourself?' she asked sarcastically.

Danny eyed her with suspicion.

''S a matter of fact, I did,' he said. 'Anyway, this ain't no easy gang to break into. First you gotta pass a test.'

'What kind of test?' she murmured apprehensively.

He moved towards her, his voice lowered to a whisper.

'You gotta steal more than twenty dollars, cash or goods, it don't make no differ.'

She hadn't imagined this 'test' was ever likely to be some harmless prank, not with Danny Feeney involved. But this was beyond belief. The fact that Denis had already passed was horrifying.

'You forced him to steal,' she said, loud enough for the couple at the next table to hear.

They turned and stared, first at her then at Danny. A deep blush rose in Danny's cheeks.

'Keep it down,' he whispered fiercely. 'I didn't force nobody. It was down to the guy himself.'

'So, who did he steal from?'

'Ah, we hit Ryan's store. Denis kept the old lady busy at the back of the store and we snatched the loot.'

She thought of old Mrs Ryan and her soft spot for Denis. It seemed to Nora that this was about as low as anyone could go.

'How much did you take?'

'Twenty-five dollars,' he told her, 'and a couple of stray nickels.'

He stretched back again and took a cigarette packet from his inside pocket.

'You still gonna talk to the cops?' he asked derisively.

'I haven't decided yet,' she said, though she knew it was out of the question now.

Danny lit his cigarette and blew the smoke at her. Her eyes stung and her throat gagged at the evil exhalation.

'I gotta warn you,' he said, 'my old man's got this neighbourhood in his pocket and he don't take no one getting in his way — or mine.'

The man sitting behind Nora began to cough. He wheeled around and eyed Danny up and down.

'Go smoke your trash somewhere else, buddy,' he rasped between coughs.

'Get outa my face, you bum,' Danny snarled. However, he had underestimated the man's long reach. In one quick movement, the man had clipped Danny's ear, knocked his hat to the ground and yanked the cigarette from between his mean little lips.

'Make yourself scarce,' the man warned him.

'You don't know who you're messing with, you dummy,' Danny yelped as he bent down to retrieve his hat.

'Hey, I'm real scared, shorty,' the man declared, nudging the lady at his side, who broke into a fit of laughter.

Danny stood up to his full height, adding an inch or two by lifting his heels off the ground. As he backed away he glanced shamefacedly at Nora who couldn't help smiling. He stuck out his forefinger in the man's direction.

'You ever heard of Lefty Feeney?' he yelled. 'Well, he's my old man.'

The woman stopped laughing.

'And mister,' Danny went on, 'I don't never forget a face.'

He slammed the door behind him. The echo rang across the silent diner. Even the screaming children had taken fright and gone suddenly quiet. After some uncomfortable shuffling about, the man behind Nora turned to his partner.

'Let's clear outa this dive.'

As they passed hurriedly by, Nora saw that his face was deathly pale. In the woman's eye tears were beginning to form.

'You had to act the big guy, didn't you,' she cried.

A small child began to wail and his lament was taken up by the other children. All eyes were now on Nora. She looked at the glass before her and her stomach turned. Too embarrassed to face down the collective gaze of the other customers she slid out from her seat and made a quick exit.

As she retraced her steps to Wash-Basin Street the feeling that she was being watched remained with her. It seemed to her that she stood out like a sore thumb among these city dwellers. The heavy twill of her dress was in stark contrast to the light skirts of the girls and women around her. Even her hair, which was long and unmanageable as ever, seemed odd compared to the smart, short cut that was the fashion here in the city. Soon this self-conscious feeling turned to something more menacing. She was gripped by an overwhelming sensation of being followed.

Quickening her stride she shot suspicious glances in all directions but found nothing to account for her fearfulness. By the time she had reached the corner of Wash-Basin Street she was almost ready to collapse. The sight of Ryan's store on the opposite side of the street didn't help. A hand touched her side and she jumped forward uttering a weak cry.

'It's only me,' Ritchie assured her.

'Did you follow me all the way?' she asked with an urgency that left Ritchie in a quandary.

'All the way from where?'

Nora folded her arms to stop them trembling but it didn't help. Her fringe was stuck to her forehead with sweat and she swept it back quickly. Her hands seemed to take on a life of their own, searching for somewhere to hide.

'I just saw you this minute,' Ritchie said. 'Are you alright?'

She wondered how much Ritchie really knew about Denis. If he knew everything it was disheartening to think he hadn't confided in her by now. If he didn't, surely it wouldn't be fair to draw him into the whole sorry mess? She decided it would be better not to ask him directly but there was something he could tell her.

'Who's Lefty Feeney?'

'Aw, Nora,' he complained. 'Don't start up on all that stuff again.'

'Who is he?' she insisted.

'He's Danny's father, you know that already, I bet.'

'But what does he do?' Nora asked. 'Why are people so afraid of him?'

'He's in the rackets, I suppose, a gangster, like.'

Ritchie turned to walk away but Nora had to know more. 'Rackets? What's that supposed to mean?'

'Aw, you know, rum-running, bank jobs, whatever pays I guess, and he's a loan shark too. He gives you money when you're in a fix but you never finish paying him off. He just keeps turning the screw. He's a no good bum.'

The truth, or what she imagined to be the truth, struck Nora like a bolt from the blue. Lefty Feeney was a loan shark and Phil had taken out a loan two years ago. Surely there was a connection. If so, there was only one way to find out.

'Where's this bank Phil works in?' she demanded. 'Can you take me there?'

'It's ten blocks from here. And Fay will be waiting for us.'

'I have to go there right now and if you don't bring me I'll find it myself.'

'But she'll be wondering what's up.'

'Maybe she will,' Nora said, 'and maybe she won't.'

He stalked away from Wash-Basin Street and she followed. Just as Nora had pretended not to be with Danny Feeney, Ritchie now refused to walk beside her. Along Melrose Ave, East 161st Street and Boscobell Ave she followed, feeling she was being watched again. She wondered quite seriously whether the madness of this city had entered her very soul, her thoughts rushing, as they did, like these busy crowds.

Just beyond a bridge over the Harlem River he pointed gruffly at an imposing building and her heart sank to see the look of cold disdain on his young face. However, she wasn't going to be stopped now. Her mind was made up.

'Don't tell him I brought you,' Ritchie said, 'I'll wait here for you.'

Nora went up ahead to a set of traffic lights where a group of people were waiting impatiently to cross. The lights turned to red and when the others began to move she joined them. Halfsway across, a car in the front of the line of traffic slipped its gear and lurched forward towards her. From behind she was grabbed and pushed away to safety. Without stopping to see who had saved her she dashed to the other side of the street.

Looking back she saw a broad-shouldered man bent in towards the driver and banging his powerful fist on the car bonnet. She didn't wait to see his face but went falteringly to the door of the First Mutual Bank.

'You looking for someone, lady?' a voice called in her ear above the clamour of traffic.

Certain she was about to come face to face with her pursuer she spun around. At first she hardly recognised Phil in his uniform, no more than she'd recognised his voice in her confusion.

'I need to talk to you,' she said evenly, gathering her strength for the confrontation ahead.

Phil's cheerfulness faded quickly. 'Let's go inside,' he said.

He brought her to a small windowless office. Switching on a table lamp he looked almost sickly in the meagre light.

'So, what's the problem,' he said, trying to seem unconcerned.

'That loan you got. Was it from Lefty Feeney?'

He sat down heavily like a wounded man.

'I guess so,' he muttered.

'So you can't warn Danny off because you're afraid of his father?'

'Something like that.'

He stared disconsolately at a bundle of papers stacked before him.

'Look, maybe I was looking for things to be wrong when I came and I'm sorry about that. But it's not my fault what I found out,' she said.

'If it was just one man I wouldn't mind,' he told her, 'but Lefty Feeney is working for a guy who runs half of New York. Can't you understand that? It's a gang of forty, maybe fifty hoods. You can't fight those odds. Believe me I've tried.'

The room was like a furnace, hardly a mouthful of air left to breathe. She found a chair and rested her weary legs. Phil's air of helplessness made her feel even more tired than she already was.

'So who's this fellow he works for?'

'Ruby,' he said, 'Harry Ruby.'

Phil was gazing at some point above Nora's head. He didn't seem to be addressing her at all, only talking aloud to himself as he continued.

'When I came out here to the States I had it tough, I can tell you. The jobs I had to take. But I stuck it out and I got by. Then Fay came along and things looked rosy but...I make one mistake, one mistake and the whole ball park comes crashing down on me.'

'You mean taking the boys in?'

'The loan, Nora. I've paid it back ten times over and the guy's still on my back. Believe me, I couldn't get the money anywhere else. I tried the bank here but I hadn't been working long enough in the place. They just wouldn't give it to me.'

'Why can't you just go out to the Midwest right now?' she asked in desperation.

'We can't disappear just like that. These guys are watching all the time.'

Nora's patience was wearing thin.

'Did you know about Denis?' she asked sharply, 'And what happened at Ryan's store?'

For all his dark good looks, Phil was a pitiful wreck of a man now. He squirmed and shifted about, looking everywhere but at Nora.

'Who told you?' he muttered.

'Danny Feeney. And if you hadn't let Denis gad around with him it would never have come to this.'

'I tried to stop him, Nora, but Lefty told me he'd up the interest some more if I got in the way of Danny's dumb little gang.'

'You should have gone to the police back then before Denis helped them rob Ryan's.'

'And what could I have told them? That the kid was running wild on the streets? What do you think they would have done? And if I told them I owed Lefty some money you know what would happen? I'd lose my job, nothing surer. A guy works in a bank and owes money to a hoodlum is out the door straight away.'

He rose to his feet and went to the door. It seemed as though he was calling a halt to this futile conversation. At the door he turned slowly. Nora could sense the struggle going on in his mind whether to say more or leave well enough alone.

'Listen, there *is* a way out of this,' he said finally. 'I don't like it but I've got to take the chance.'

'What will you have to do?'

'That's between me and Lefty,' he told her, 'You better leave now, I've got enough problems already. The manager's gonna be asking questions if I don't get back out front.'

In spite of herself, Nora was moved to pity. Phil may have been foolish to take out the loan but he'd done it for her brothers. Surely it wasn't his fault that he'd gone to the wrong person for the money. The terrible consequences were not of his own making. Whatever his faults, his heart was in the right place.

'If there was another way I'd try it,' Phil said, 'Or...or if there was someone else who could help us.... When I was a kid I used to believe there was a guardian angel watching over me. I guess I left him behind in Dublin. And there's no angels in this city.'

Like an image on a cinema screen the face of the mysterious stranger from the ship flashed before Nora's eyes. He made an unlikely angel with his twitching left eye. It was too preposterous to give even a second thought. She had no idea who the stranger was or where he lived and for all she knew he might be another of the gangsters, destroying innocent lives. Hadn't Hans discovered a gun in his henchman's pocket?

There was only one thing she knew for certain about him, apart from his first name, Vincent. He was the one who'd asked that she be auditioned. So, they must know who he is at the... Before she had even formed the words in her mind, she spoke.

'Do you know where the LaFonde Musical Foundation is?'

CHAPTER 11

For half an hour she travelled across the city in a taxi. Phil had called it for her, though she'd hadn't explained her true purpose in going to the Foundation. As for Ritchie, he didn't want to know what she was up to. When she told him she had another call to make he spat out a lump of that awful gum stuff the boys were always chewing, and walked away. He didn't tell her to take care. He said nothing at all.

As the taxi inched forward in the early afternoon rush she slipped off the shoes from her aching feet. The imitation pearl necklace, given to her by the boys, was tight as a hangman's noose around her neck. She took it off and slipped it into her pocket. She made a secret promise to herself not to wear it again until all these problems were ironed out and she and her brothers were friends again. Even as she made this promise she began to doubt whether that time would ever come.

The stately frontage of the Musical Foundation building seemed depressingly familiar. It was, in fact, almost a replica of the bathhouse on Wash-Basin Street. The same grand tiered entrance led to similar Romanesque columns. Above, an inscription was chiselled into the grey stone. Only the words 'La Musique' meant anything to Nora. The rest might as well have been some message of warning, so apprehensive did she feel.

Inside, the place glistened with highly-polished white

marble; the floors, the walls, the wide sweeping staircase. For a musical academy it was forbiddingly silent.

The pale-faced woman at the reception desk was herself like a marble statue. Even as Nora's footsteps echoed to the heights, the receptionist didn't give her so much as a glance. With great trepidation Nora approached, clearing her throat loudly to no avail.

'Excuse me,' she whispered.

The woman raised only her eyes. Her face was not as perfect as it had seemed from a distance. Above her wrinkled forehead the woman's blonde hair seemed out of place, like it was dyed or was, perhaps, a wig.

'Do you have an appointment to call?'

The foreigness of her accent made the silent academy seem even stranger still.

'Not exactly,' Nora replied.

'You are wasting my time then,' the blonde lady said, turning her attention once again to the paperback novel before her.

'I got a letter,' Nora explained, 'asking me to come for an audition.'

'From whom?'

'I...I couldn't read the signature, I'm sorry.'

Without looking up the woman reached a deeply-veined hand towards Nora. It was delicate and frail as though crafted in bone china.

'You have the letter?' she asked, flicking over a page of her book.

'No,' Nora said desperately, 'I mean I forgot to bring it with me.'

The woman shrugged her shoulders. She had nothing more to say. Nora was getting vexed and for a moment thought about rushing up the wide staircase to find someone else to speak to, someone less forbidding who might tell her who the stranger was.

'It's important,' Nora cried, 'I've come all the way from Ireland and I don't have much time here.'

At last, the woman's calm air of disdain was ruffled.

'I will see what I can do,' she said and rose majestically from her seat. 'Your name is?'

'Nora Canavan. If you could just tell me...'

Nora stared in wonder as the receptionist made her way to the foot of the expansive stairs. She was, without doubt, the tallest woman Nora had ever seen. Despite her stature she walked with all the grace of a ballerina.

In a matter of minutes she had appeared again at the top of the stairs followed by a balding man who was muttering wildly to himself. He seemed small and pudgy beside the gaunt, alabaster lady but then anyone would have.

'Highly irregular,' he blustered. 'From the beginning it is highly irregular with this hideous man and now she comes without the appointment.'

He squinted half-blindly in Nora's direction. The woman crooked her long finger and Nora ascended, her legs heavy and threatening to give out at any moment.

When she'd reached the top the perspiration was streaming down her face again despite the coolness of the marbled interior. She felt decidedly faint. Walking alongside the tall lady she followed the examiner and tried to speak.

'I just want to...find out who...' she stuttered but the woman looked straight ahead as if she hadn't heard.

When the woman did speak, Nora wondered if she'd only imagined it. 'Don't be afraid of that silly old man,' was what she thought she heard.

The place was so hushed that she expected at any moment to see a nun or a cowled monk appear. Instead she heard, ever so faintly, a distant suggestion of music from above. It was like the music of some cold heaven.

Soon she was seated at a desk in a white, brightly-lit room. She was finding it difficult to concentrate, her mind unable to keep up with the raging current of the day's events.

'I'm very tired,' she said, 'You see, I only came here to...'

'If you are unwell, you should not be here,' the man said. 'In fact, you should not be here this day. And now, you offer the excuses.'

His head seemed to bob around like a ball thrown in the sea. Nora's arms fell to her side. She was about to tell him she was going to be sick when the bright room turned first to grey and then darkness descended upon her.

When she came to, she was lying on the floor beside a toppled chair. Her head was nestled in the tall lady's lap. From behind came the sound of impatient little footsteps pacing up and down the room.

'Will you please stop marching around and help the girl to her seat,' the woman demanded.

All Nora wanted to do was escape this curious couple and their marbled fortress. It seemed unlikely that this man would answer any question of hers. He obviously had little time for the stranger whom she supposed he was referring to when he'd mentioned 'this hideous man'. Her desire to leave seemed to be matched by his desire to be rid of her.

'In the circumstances,' he announced, 'an audition would not be in your interests, no?'

Nora was all set to agree but the woman intervened.

'You will have,' she told Nora, 'ten minutes to rest and prepare yourself.'

'Mais non,' the man cried, 'It is impossible.'

'*You* are impossible,' the woman said tersely and turned to Nora. 'My husband will return shortly and he *will* listen.'

Too weak to protest, Nora followed the examiner's wife to the far end of the room. Only now did she realise that there was a piano there. Like everything else in the place it was gleaming white.

'I'm not used to playing the grand piano,' Nora objected, 'Only on the ship and that was just three or four times...'

She knew this wasn't making any sense to the others and thought it pointless to explain any further.

'Grand piano. Grand piano,' the examiner declared, 'Such musical ignorance.'

Nora looked at him and then at the piano. It had the shape of a grand piano though it wasn't quite as large as the one in the lounge of the SS *Bremen*.

'This is a boudoir piano, my dear,' he announced, stroking the instrument like it was a favourite pet, 'not a grand piano.'

'Not everyone has had a spoilt youth,' his wife said witheringly and he retreated in a huff from the piano.

The woman raised the piano lid and sat Nora down at the keys. The coldness with which she'd met Nora had evaporated. Her icy pallor had somehow softened too and her cheeks glowed with an unexpected warmth.

'You must try to relax,' she said.

'But there's something I wanted to ask...'

'If you have questions you may ask them later. Now, do as I do.'

'But...'

'Please,' the woman insisted, 'Breathe...like this.'

She drew in long, deep breaths and released them slowly. Of all the peculiar situations Nora had found herself in, this had to be the strangest. Here she was, sitting at a resplendently white piano in a bright, luminous room alongside the tallest, most exotic woman she'd ever laid eyes on, breathing in and out in unison. The spaces all around were filled with a ghostly echo like waves lapping on some far-off shore. Stranger still was the fact that the trick seemed to be working.

'Now, what will you play for my dear husband?'

'It wouldn't make any difference what I played for that

fellow. Anyway, I didn't really come to...'

'Of course it will make a difference. It is absolutely critical what you decide to play.'

There seemed to be no choice now but to go through with the audition. Besides, she felt grateful to the tall woman for her kindness and sure that she would soon find out from her who the stranger was.

'I don't have any music with me,' she said.

'Here, we have everything, don't worry.'

Nora remembered the piece that had so impressed the stranger. 'Do you have *Trois Gymnopedies* by Satie?'

'Yes,' the woman said uncertainly, 'but my husband is not a great lover of these Modernists. I would suggest Bach and a little Chopin. It is better to have a more clear-cut distinction between invention and Romanticism. My husband, you see, is a simple man.'

The explanation was lost on Nora but she did know some pieces by these composers and the woman went away to find the sheet music for her. Very hesitantly she tried some major and minor scales. The piano had that same instant response to her touch as the grand piano she'd played on. She realised that this audition meant nothing to her since she had no intention of studying in this place even if it went right. She was going ahead only because if she didn't, they would both be too angry with her even to listen to her question.

The examiner, now wearing a long black cape over his suit, made a grand entrance. He tossed her the sheet music with a dismissive grunt. Pulling a chair across the marble floor he sat in the centre of the room.

'At least you have made a reasonable choice of music. If a little sombre for one so young.'

'I'm nearly sixteen, actually.'

'Ah, a woman of the world, then,' he sneered.

Ignoring his remark, Nora began and though it was almost

two weeks since she'd played either piece she sailed through them with growing confidence. All the emotions of these last few days poured into her playing. The joy and disappointment, the hurt and anger, the despair and finally and above all, the hope she clung to, the absolute refusal to give in. The bright room seemed even more radiant in the afterglow of her performance.

The examiner, when she looked over at him, was fumbling with an oversized handkerchief. There was a definite hint of moisture in his eyes but his face was as stern as ever.

'A slight tendency to elaborate,' was his verdict.

'Thank you,' Nora said brusquely.

'I have, you see, a little motto, which has served me very well,' he went on, 'Talent is a mere footsoldier. It is the genius, as it were, of the General that will prevail. Now, I must decide in which category you belong.'

'How long will that take?'

'Who can say? But I must remind you that *nobody* influences my decision, no matter how great their financial contribution to my humble Foundation.'

Humble, Nora thought. This fellow wouldn't recognise humility if it jumped up and bit him. He stood up and showed her to the door. He seemed in such a hurry to see the back of her that she was altogether certain she would be getting no offer to study in this cold palace. She wasn't particularly disappointed but she still had her question to ask.

'Excuse me,' she began, 'but who exactly asked you to audition me?'

'You don't know this?' he asked suspiciously and considering the matter for a while, added, 'Well then...he clearly has his reasons not to tell you and if this is so I cannot help. He is not the kind of man to be trifled with.'

'But I want to thank him. That's all.'

'If he should want you to know his identity, he will no

doubt make himself known to you. Now, I really am quite busy,' he said, closing the door in her face.

She felt like kicking the door in her frustration but instead moved away quickly to find his wife. However, when she reached the bottom of the staircase a different woman was sitting at the reception desk.

'Could I speak to the...the tall lady?'

'I'm afraid the Countess has just left. Can I help you?'

Nora was already on her way to the front door. Emerging on to the sweltering street she was certain she saw the Countess disappear around the street corner to her right. She ran along the sidewalk and turned first one corner and then another and another but eventually she lost sight of the woman entirely.

She searched in her pockets for the money Phil had given her for the taxi-ride back to Wash-Basin Street. It was nowhere to be found. To her consternation, she discovered that the pearl necklace that the boys had given her was missing too. It occurred to her that they must have fallen from her pocket when she'd fainted and she decided to go back to the Foundation building.

In her haste to catch up with the Countess, however, she'd become completely lost. Not one of the passersby she asked had ever heard of the Foundation, some refused even to answer her.

In desperation she searched for a policeman but none was to be found. The noise and heat of the city began to close in on her as she stumbled along in confusion. Then a voice intruded on her panic. She couldn't hear his words but as she glanced sideways she saw the dark suit, the black shirt and the white tie.

It wasn't Danny, but as soon as he spoke it was clear he was one of the Feeney gang.

'Listen, lady,' he growled, 'I got two things to say to you.

Stay away from Danny Feeney and stop asking questions, see?'

He pushed her roughly against a shop window and raised his fist towards her. In an instant, the man lay stretched out on the pavement, hit from behind by a vaguely familiar broad-shouldered character. Her rescuer was about to speak to her but she ran, pushing her way through the crowds.

She raced against the stream of humanity until someone took hold of her arm. She stifled a scream as she looked up along the line of five silver buttons, the badge initialled NYPD and the peaked hat of a tall, young policeman.

CHAPTER 12

'Lost?' the police officer asked. 'You sure you ain't snatched somethin'?'

Nora scanned the passersby for any sign of the two men but they had disappeared. Then, realising what the officer had just said to her she eyed him angrily.

'How dare you call me a thief,' she snapped and added foolishly, as if it proved her innocence, 'I'm from Ireland.'

'So what's a pretty young Irish girl doing wandering the streets of New York?'

She told him she was on holiday at Wash-Basin Street in Mott Haven, The Bronx, that she'd come out for a walk and lost her way.

'I'll take you there. It's not so far,' he offered.

For a moment she worried about how Denis would react if he saw her arriving home with a policeman. Then again, maybe a real fright was what he needed.

'Thanks,' she said and they set off through the thronged pavements.

'Sergeant Novak's the name, by the way. What's yours?'

As she told him a warning voice entered her head not to let him know too much about herself.

'A wonderful city, New York, ain't it?' he declared as they went along.

'As far as I can see it's full of gangsters,' Nora said and

instantly regretted it.

'There's a few of them about, sure,' he told her with a look of suspicion, 'but for every one hoodlum there's a hundred, a thousand hard-working folk from every corner of the wide earth making a better living than they ever could in their home country. Maybe there's more beautiful places to live in but you can't eat pretty views.'

She thought this was probably true but it wasn't much consolation when you were already entangled in the snares of the criminals, no matter how few of them there were.

They arrived, at last, at the corner of Wash-Basin Street.

'I'll be fine now,' Nora said, 'I know where I am. Thanks very much.'

'Hey, I'll have to say hello to your folks.'

'They won't be in,' she objected, 'They'll be at work and the boys won't be home from school yet.'

'Well, I wouldn't say no to a coffee after that walk,' he grinned, 'How about it?'

She led him to the apartment house hoping against hope that Fay had gone out searching for her. However, it was Fay who answered her half-hearted knock on the door.

'Nora,' she cried, her eyes red and moist, 'We thought something terrible must have happened to you.'

When she saw Sergeant Novak she swayed visibly as if ready to collapse. Denis appeared from behind her, took one look and bolted for his room.

'I got lost,' Nora said, 'I'm sorry.'

'Found her over on West 230th Street,' the sergeant told Fay, 'and hey, tell the kid I ain't gonna arrest him.'

Fay was panic-stricken. The police officer stopped laughing and with great embarrassment turned to go. Nora felt sorry for the good-natured fellow.

'Won't you have a cup of coffee?' she asked.

'Yeah. Sure, Officer. I should've asked you in. I was so

worried, you know,' Fay muttered.

'Hey, it's alright.' Novak laughed as he turned to go. 'I guess the uniform scares the kids sometimes. A hazard of the job.'

'Thanks again,' Nora called after him.

'You take care now, Nora,' he said with a grin. 'Don't go chasing the guys around town. Let them chase you.'

She was reminded of John Moloney and his teasing ways. Right now she would gladly have enlisted John's help but he was miles away on tour with the hurling party. It was a shock to her to think she could ever have imagined wanting him to be around.

Fay closed the door of the apartment on his retreating footsteps and pressed her back against it. Nora didn't know where to look or what to do. Her aunt was shaking all over. No amount of make-up could hide the sickly greyness of her cheeks.

'I asked you to stay on Wash-Basin Street,' she said. 'I've been down to Ryan's three times and you never showed up there.'

There was certainly concern in her voice but Nora thought it was a bit late now for that. She had no intention of letting herself feel guilty after her efforts to find the stranger.

'It wasn't my fault,' she said.

'So whose fault was it?'

'If Denis wasn't in this mess,' Nora answered, 'I wouldn't have had to follow Danny Feeney and spend the morning running around this stinking city.'

'What're you playin' at? Phil told you he's doin' what he can to work this thing out. What more do you want?'

'If my father knew what was going on, or Aunt Molly or Peter, they'd have the lads out of here very fast.'

They stood head to head, both with hands on hips, defying each other. The sheer venom of their stand-up argument frightened them both. But there was no giving in, no letting up.

'Nobody's going to take those kids from me,' Fay shouted, 'Do you hear me, *nobody*!'

'You might not have any choice.'

Nora was saying things now she hardly understood herself, and she wasn't finished yet.

'You don't know the half of what's going on right under your powdered nose. But I know. That creepy little Feeney fellow told me.'

Suddenly there was a cry from the boys' bedroom and Denis swung open the door.

'Shut up, Nora,' he warned. 'You just shut your trap and leave us all alone.'

Behind him, Ritchie was pleading with all of them to stop. It was already too late. The atmosphere in the apartment was bitter and with every breath each one of them became more enraged.

'Do you want to tell your precious Auntie Fay about Ryan's store?' Nora snapped, 'Or will I?'

Denis banged his foot on the floor. On the sideboard his trophies swayed and almost fell over.

'I don't know nothing about who robbed Ryan's,' he yelled and realising she hadn't mentioned a robbery, punched the wall.

One of Phil's framed pictures fell and the glass shattered with a bang on the floor. He helped the frame on its way with a vengeful kick.

'Denis,' Fay uttered weakly, 'Oh, my God, Denis.'

Seeing Fay's distress, Denis' tough facade began to crumble. Brushing past Nora he went to his aunt and buried his head in her arms. Nora stood alone as Fay comforted him. She felt even more lost than she had done in the city streets earlier. She looked over at Ritchie, her eyes crying out to him to come to her side. He moved closer but stopped short just beyond her reach.

'I swear, Fay,' Denis was crying, 'I couldn't help it. They roped me in. Danny was beating up on me, him and his gang.'

Nora wasn't convinced by this outburst.

'So how come Ritchie didn't get caught up?' she asked. 'You're only making excuses for yourself.'

He ignored her. Whatever explaining he was going to do it was for Fay's benefit only.

'*You* believe me, don't you, Fay?' he pleaded. 'They wanted me 'cause I win all those stupid races at school. So, Danny thought I'd be good for his gang and he made me help him rob Ryan's. But I didn't want to, I swear. Mrs Ryan's real nice to me. I really didn't want to do it.'

'Does Phil know about this?' Fay asked Denis softly.

'Yes, he does,' Nora interrupted.

Denis didn't seem to care anymore what Nora thought of him. Only Fay, it seemed, mattered to him. And Phil.

'I should've told you, Fay,' he said, 'but I was afraid, 'specially after what Danny said to me when we got out of Ryan's.'

Now, at least, both Fay and Nora were as one, trembling in anticipation.

'What did Danny say?' Fay asked calmly.

'He said Phil would have to do whatever Danny's father wanted now or they'd snitch on me. I don't know what he meant. I told him Phil was paying off the loan but he only laughed at me. He said that kind of money was just peanuts, that his father had bigger plans.'

A sickening quietude descended on the apartment. Each one of them was keenly aware that whatever Danny's father expected Phil to do, it spelt only danger. There was no energy left in any of them to continue the argument. They could only wait for Phil to return home. Fay had a dinner ready but food was the last thing on their minds right now. They took turns sitting and pacing the floor and glancing at the clock on the wall.

Half an hour after Phil's usual time of arrival Ritchie went down the apartment house stairs. When he came back he simply shook his head disconsolately. Some time later, it was Denis' turn to escape the stifling silence. He too returned with the same grim nod of desperation.

Darkness fell and they sat in the half-light from the street. It was as if they wanted to hide from each other the mounting strain on their faces. Finally, they heard Phil's heavy tread on the stairway. Fay went and turned on the light. As soon as he appeared on the landing she ran to him and wrapped her arms around his waist.

'See the conquering hero comes,' he laughed queerly.

It was no time for poetry. The words dropped like stones in the troubled waters of their hearts. He stepped inside and only now could Nora see what had upset Fay so much. The left side of Phil's face was badly bruised and swollen. On his cheek there was a dark smudge of blood. The sleeve of his leather jacket was torn at the elbow and the front of his shirt was ripped open, revealing horrific bruises. Worst of all though was the almost crazed look in his eyes contrasting so strangely with his calm smile.

'I've just had a friendly chat with Lefty Feeney and a couple of his pals,' he said.

Choked with fear, they waited to hear more. Phil reached his favourite chair, the one by the radio, and his legs folded under him as he dropped in a crumpled heap onto the soft cushion.

'Nora's told me about Denis and Ryan's store,' Fay said, kneeling beside him.

'I was trying to protect you, Fay,' he whispered, 'Trying to smooth it all over. You got enough on your plate already.'

Denis uttered a groan of misery.

'It's alright, Denis,' Phil told him, 'The guy was going to corner me one way or the other.'

They waited to hear what had happened, their eyes trans-fixed by his glassy stare.

'They picked me up a few blocks from the bank,' he explained, 'They were talking about some cop calling here.'

Nora looked guiltily at Fay but her aunt shook her head as if to reassure her.

'We get to this shed down the docks and they begin to work me over. Next thing a couple of guys break in with guns. First, I thought it was the cops but they told me to hightail it outa there. I don't ask questions, I just leg it... It's all crazy.'

Nora wondered who wanted to rescue both herself and Phil from the Feeney gang. The thought had no sooner oc-curred to her when she was distracted by Phil's laughter — the despairing laughter of a sad-faced clown.

'Let's clean you up,' Fay said. 'Nora, can you boil some water and maybe heat up the dinner?'

Nora was glad to help Fay calm the situation. It felt good to be doing something after the hours of motionless silence. In the kitchen she made more noise than she needed to with the pots and pans. She had good reason. The moans of pain coming from Phil's room were sending the boys into a new frenzy of panic. The clamour Nora conjured up covered some of the evidence of his suffering, at least.

Soon, Fay emerged from the bedroom. In spite of their efforts to help tidy up after the dinner which they'd barely touched, she insisted on the boys going to bed. They drifted away miserably but Nora wasn't quite sure what she should do. From the bedroom Phil's sighs of discomfort were plain to hear.

'Maybe you should go back in to him, and I can finish up this lot.'

'No!' Fay cried, 'Just go...just...'

A greasy plate slipped from her hands and Nora caught it before it hit the floor. Fay turned to the sink, her body heaving. Nora almost brought herself to reach across and touch her shoulder but into her mind flashed an inexplicable warning. Something is going to happen to me next, it said. Her stomach tightened. She felt selfish thinking about herself when there was so much trouble already going on all around her. But the warning rang on.

'He's going to need a doctor,' Fay murmured. 'They broke his ribs again.'

'Again?'

'Yeah, he just told me now. They beat up on him a while back. He told us back then it happened when some guys tried to rob the bank. We thought he was a real hero,' she smiled sadly, 'but I don't care about all that, he'll always be a hero to me.'

At the apartment door she slipped a coat over her dressing-gown and absentmindedly began to match the wrong buttons with the wrong holes. Nora helped her to tie it up.

'I'll come with you,' she offered.

'Better not. You can keep an eye on the kids, OK? If Phil's looking for me, I'm in the lady's room, right?'

Nora realised that going out into the night could be dangerous. There was no knowing what Feeney would get up to next and as Phil had made clear he was watching all the time.

'Be careful,' she said.

'They've got a phone next door,' Fay explained, 'Don't go worrying yourself.'

Fay left and Nora stood in the sitting room, the ticking clock slowly counting out the seconds like it was tired of trying. Then, without warning, Ritchie burst into the room and set time racing again.

'Nora, he's gonna do something stupid,' he exclaimed, 'Stop him, Nora! Don't let him go!'

CHAPTER 13

Denis already had one foot on the fire escape when Nora reached him. She pulled him back in and pushed him on to his bed. He sat quietly, refusing to fight back. His face was set hard in a fierce look of determination, a look that reminded Nora of an acrobat in a travelling circus she'd once seen. Back then she couldn't keep her eyes from that man's face, drained of all fear, of any sense of danger in that moment before the dive into the air. But the acrobat had another man to catch him as he fell. Somehow, Nora guessed she would be the one to save Denis from plummeting to the ground.

'After all this,' she cried in disbelief, 'you still want to meet your so-called friend. How could you?'

'He ain't no friend of mine.'

'Ask him what he's got in his pocket, Nora,' Ritchie said.

'Aw, shut up,' Denis snapped.

'Denis?'

'I'm gonna teach Danny a lesson,' Denis muttered. 'He's gonna get his.'

Catching him by his shirt front, Nora lifted him from the bed. He hung limply before her, offering no resistance, still fixed in his determined trance. Nora was tempted to slap his face and break the spell but as if he'd read her mind, he spoke.

'Why don't you belt me? That's what everyone wants to do. It's what I deserve, isn't it?'

'Empty your pockets,' Nora insisted.

'There's nothing to empty.'

'You know there is,' Ritchie said and moved alongside Denis.

'Stay out of it, Ritchie,' Denis warned, 'You already told her about the Foggy Club, stool-pigeon.'

Ritchie reached towards the inside pocket of his brother's jacket. He seemed to know exactly what he was looking for and where to find it. Denis pushed his hand away but as he did Nora grabbed her chance. She plunged her left hand into the pocket and lurched back with an anguished gasp.

Blood trickled from a slender gash on the palm of her hand. But more frightening still was the sense that she couldn't move her fingers. In her mind she imagined some muscle, some sinew or nerve had been sliced through. She stared at the open wound as if her whole future was draining away in the bright red rivulets filling out the palm and spilling, drop by drop, to the floor.

Ritchie ran to the kitchen and grabbed a clean tea towel. Sneaking into the bedroom where Phil slept fitfully, he got the bandages and disinfectant he'd seen Fay bring in there. When he got back, Nora was still standing in the same spot. Below her, a purplish stain was spreading on the dark-flowered carpet. Beside it lay the razor-sharp steak knife which had done the damage. Denis' eyes were riveted to Nora's hand but he couldn't move.

'Don't just stand there,' Ritchie ordered him, 'Help me, OK?'

When the blood was cleaned away the fine inch-long line of the cut became clear. It seemed too slight to cause the kind of damage Nora had feared and yet she couldn't even begin to try moving her fingers. Pale-faced but calm, Ritchie carefully dabbed the stinging disinfectant along the scarlet edges of the wound. Denis tried to help but his hands were too unsteady. He went and sat on his bed gripping his arms across his front.

As for Nora, she felt no pain now, only a curious sense of disappointment as if something had been stolen from her. Ritchie tied the bandage as best he could and sat her down on his bed. Nora drew her hand to her stomach and held it like it was a broken doll.

'It'll be alright,' she said, 'Fay's gone to get a doctor for Phil. He can look at it.'

Now that she remembered Fay a vague sense of urgency reached through her clouded mind. It was difficult to guess how long she'd been gone but it seemed an age.

'Ritchie, will you go down and keep an eye out for Fay?' she asked, 'And thanks, I don't know what I'd have done if you hadn't kept your head.'

Ritchie shrugged shyly and went out, leaving Nora and Denis sitting on opposite beds. Between them, the mere three feet of space seemed like a chasm that would never again be crossed.

Denis fell on his knees at her feet. The chilling reminder of her spilled blood was damp against his trouser legs. His head cushioned on her lap, he cried helplessly.

'I'm sorry, Nora,' he sniffled, 'I'm so sorry.'

She ran her good hand through his hair. For a moment she was sure the feeling was returning to her other hand. The fingers moved of their own accord in a painful spasm.

'I love you,' he cried. 'God, I missed you so much. I don't know what I'll do when you go...when you have to go again. And now you hate me. You'll never want to see me again.'

'I don't hate you,' she sighed.

With a supreme effort she spread her fingers wide but the bandage slipped off and the wound gaped open. She stared at her bloodied palm and wondered how the slit edges would ever join up again. She remembered the tall crucifix in the churchyard at home, the vivid red paint on the nailed hands. And Fr Scanlon standing before it at the end of the Corpus Christi procession talking about the great sacrifice Christ had made for Man. Was this, she wondered, her 'sacrifice' for her brothers' affection?

Outside in the sitting room the apartment door opened and Denis jumped to his feet, wiping his tears in embarrassment. Fay rushed in followed by a thick-spectacled, elderly man.

'What were you playing at Denis?' she exclaimed as she took Nora's wounded hand in hers.

'It's nothing,' Nora said, 'Phil needs the doctor more than I do.'

The doctor looked around uncomfortably and his gaze descended on the little pool of blood and the jagged-edged knife on the floor. Nora could see he was wondering what kind of family this was. She wanted to explain that it wasn't like it seemed but he went about his task with such ill-humour that she didn't, in the end, care what he thought.

When the bandage was unrolled, the skin of her palm was already curiously white. Wrinkled and loose, it was like a glove that didn't fit her hand anymore. He considered the wound in a detached way. Nora knew he had probably seen worse injuries in his time but a little sympathy would have helped.

'Can you move the fingers?' he asked brusquely.

'I think so,' she muttered.

'You think so or you know so, which is it kid?'

'I'm not sure if I shou...'

'She's not sure if she should move her fingers,' he complained to no one in particular. 'Try.'

'I have tried,' she moaned, 'and it hurts.'

'It would,' he said sarcastically.

He took her hand roughly and bent each finger. Each time

she winced in agony and when he got to the small finger she'd had enough and pulled away from him.

'Take it easy, Doc,' Fay pleaded, biting her lip at the thought of Nora's discomfort.

'You telling me how to do my job?' he barked. 'I don't appreciate being hauled out of bed and I don't need anyone telling me what to do. I've seen it all before, lady.'

He bent down to examine Nora's hand close up, peering at it, his glasses a mere inch from her palm. His breath was warm and uncomfortably moist but she didn't dare draw back from him again. After too many long, agonising minutes he straightened up once more.

'It don't seem so bad,' he declared. 'Reckon I'll go and stitch it up. Don't appear to be no damage underneath. I guess you won't be doin' no sewin' for a few days but that's about it. Nothin' serious.'

'You're wrong,' Nora insisted, 'It doesn't feel right.'

The doctor glowered at her and turned to Fay.

'Where's the other patient?'

On the bed opposite Nora, Denis curled up and groaned quietly. Nora felt like she was falling clean through the air. The doctor didn't know what he was doing, she was sure of it. She closed her eyes and though she felt a queer sensation of drifting slowly away, the conversation above her seemed, if anything, louder than before. Below their words she thought she could hear music and she tried to blot it from her mind. A little chant started up, breaking down the insistent melody. It was Denis, repeating over and over, 'No, no, no.'

'Is there some way we can check this out,' Fay was saying, 'just so's we can be sure?'

'Not unless you got a big cash flow,' the doctor answered huffily. 'The kid's panicked is all.'

'She seems pretty certain there's a problem.'

Even as she floated in her strange netherworld, Nora could

sense the doctor's irritation.

'If the kid's hand is so awful important,' he sneered, 'why not take her to some big-time specialist. Cost you a hundred bucks just to jump the queue and that's just for starters. Only Rockefellers and hoodlums can pay these prices. Guy out at Brimstead Private Clinic. Stoneleigh's the name. Sell every last thing you got and go see him but he'll tell you the same thing I told you.'

As he began to stitch her wound Nora wanted to cry out that he was making a big mistake. She had no idea why but the certainty was overwhelming when the last stitch was completed that the passage to all she held dear was being closed off with a piece of thread.

When the doctor left to see Phil she didn't open her eyes. She welcomed the dark and thought she understood how Aunt Molly could accept it so easily. In many ways it was a better place to be in. You didn't have to see the world that had been so cruel to you or be reminded of the things it had denied you. Even so, she knew there was no way to banish the music from her heart and mind. It would always be there to haunt her.

She heard Denis move from his bed and, for a brief moment, felt his breath on her forehead. He stepped back and paused in the dead silence. Something brushed along the floor. His hand.

'Put it down,' she said.

A light thud on the floor told her he'd dropped the knife. He left quietly without a word.

Now that she was alone the music in her head became more and more insistent, refusing to be ignored. In her turmoil she began to feel a terrible hatred rise up in her.

It began with all the instruments of music which seemed to scream and squeal and bellow discordantly at her. She imagined herself in a room full of violins, French horns, clarinets, double basses, pianos, and smashing everything to bits.

Then her venom turned to people. The evil Feeney and Ruby, whose faces she had to create for herself; Danny Feeney too, with his ridiculous suit. But it didn't stop there. Denis was here and she was slapping his face time and again. Phil took a beating from her too for his stupidity in getting involved with Lefty Feeney. Even Uncle Peter back home in Tipperary wasn't safe from her vengeful sweep. Why, she screamed silently, did you send me to this place? The doctor too with his stubbornness felt her fury.

And still the music went on. She sat up in the bed, pleading with the melody to end and to stop torturing her. On the very point of giving up on her sanity she paused and all at once understood.

The music hadn't come to make her even more miserable. It had come to remind her of something only she'd been too busy taking quiet revenge on the world. Now the message came loud and clear. Remember Alec. Remember his ravaged hand and the middle finger torn away in the Great War. Remember what he'd said. There is always a way, if the music is in your soul, there will always be a way to release it.

At this moment it was impossible to imagine what that way might be. If she couldn't play the piano what else could there be? Was there some other instrument? None came to mind. Could she, perhaps, create her own music for others to play? The idea seemed too grand by far and yet she knew that there were times these past two years when the music in her mind wasn't always simply some melody she'd heard elsewhere.

As vague as these hopes were they lifted her spirits. She had never been defeated by misfortune before and somehow she knew she wasn't going to be defeated this time.

She stood up expecting to feel groggy after her ordeal. She

felt as though she were floating as she entered the sitting room, where the boys looked at her aghast.

'Nora,' Fay declared, 'you should be resting.'

'I'm fine. How's Phil?'

'A couple of bruised ribs. He's got to lie up for a few days.'

Denis got up from his chair and Nora could see he was trying to bring himself to talk to her. She knew that forgiveness would have to start some time but she felt suddenly unwilling to make it easy for him. Instead of telling him that it was alright, that there was no need to say anything, she waited and watched him a little too coldly. He turned even more pale than he already was. Nora felt the queerest sensation that something small and evil was growing in the depths of her wound, some throbbing thing.

'Right, you guys,' Fay announced. 'Better hit the sack.'

There were no objections. The boys said their goodnights and Ritchie followed Denis to their room. At the door he turned and spoke quietly, as if he didn't want Denis to hear.

'Everything's gonna work out, ain't it, Nora?'

She nodded and he seemed happy enough with that.

For a while she and Fay sat quietly near the window staring out at the night sky. The harsh, clashing music had passed from Nora's mind and all the hatred too.

'You seem so calm,' Fay said. 'I'm sure I'd have gone half-crazy if it happened to me.'

'I'm not really. Maybe I did just panic.'

But it wasn't that simple, not with this ill-omened tremor.

'I guess so. But I don't trust that guy.'

A lorry passed on the street below making the glass in the window vibrate into music. Nora decided it made a very low A sharp. It seemed like there was music in everything just waiting to be written down. Maybe her idea about composing wasn't so insane after all?

'Is there any chance at all,' Fay asked, 'that your Uncle

Peter could get this money together? I mean it's your life the piano, I know it is. Your father writes to Phil all the time about how talented you are. That doctor is nothing but a quack, he couldn't fix up a horse never mind a human being.'

'Peter doesn't have that kind of money,' Nora insisted, 'and even if he had I wouldn't ask him. He's done enough for me already.'

'But he's got a store and a cinema. He must be rolling in it.'

'It's not New York, Fay, it's a small town. Anything he does have will go on Molly's operation.'

'There's got to be something we can do.'

Nora was beginning to feel perplexed by the conversation. She was the one whose future was threatened and yet it was Fay who was doing all the worrying. Her aunt's delicate face looked almost ugly it was so twisted and miserable. Fay had reached the point where she could take no more.

'I been bad luck since the day I was born, Nora,' she whimpered, 'and it rubs off on everyone I ever meet.'

Nora listened in growing amazement and admiration to the real story of the sad little girl behind the smart city woman.

And as her aunt spoke Nora stumbled on the discovery that would, in a matter of hours, change everything.

CHAPTER 14

If Nora had, at first, thought Fay was exaggerating when she spoke of her bad luck she was soon convinced otherwise. Fay's life had been unbelievably difficult. In fact, Nora mused, it was nothing short of a miracle that she had survived it at all. Before she'd met Fay she'd imagined she'd be like her mother in some way. As her story emerged it seemed she had more than a little in common with Nora herself.

'I never knew my own folks,' Fay began. 'They left me at an orphanage upstate. It was a living hell but I guess I would have made a hell of it anyway. When you been hurt in here you don't appreciate kindness and there was some in that place. I guess you're afraid if you get to like someone they'll just walk out on you. So I got to be a rebel and when I was fourteen they were more than glad to get rid of me. I made tracks for New York in double-quick time.'

It was difficult for Nora to disguise her expression of surprise and dismay. The truth was so very different from her imaginings.

'Pretty soon I'd gone way out of line. The things I did to survive, no one should have to do. By the time I'd reached seventeen I could drink any guy under the table. Then one morning I woke with this awful hangover and I knew I was killing myself. So, I decided to go straight, no more bars or any of that old stuff. I moved to a different part of town where nobody knew me. Spent my last few dollars on a new dress and some make-up and got myself a job in a fashion store.'

For the first time since she'd begun talking she looked directly into Nora's eyes. It was a look of pleading, not for sympathy but for understanding.

'Maybe you think that kind of stuff is too important to me. Clothes, face paints. But when you've worn nothing but grubby old sacks of things until you were fourteen and every other kid in the orphanage is wearing the same trash, these things matter. They give you back your self-respect. You look good so you feel good and you think, hey, it don't matter where you came outa. You ain't just a number anymore, you're a person.'

Fay was already brightening up a little. Nora drew her chair closer. She offered her hand to her aunt. The same gesture that, not long before, had so annoyed her, came naturally to Nora now.

'Well, for a long time, my luck held out. I was four years in the store and they'd moved me into the cosmetics department. Believe it or not I was the supervisor and things were really looking up. Then the trouble started again. The owner's son came to work in the store and he took a fancy to me. I didn't mind, he seemed an OK guy. But the other girls didn't like it one bit so they got together and found out, I don't know how, about my past. They got the word to this guy and, boy, did he drop me fast. I hit the bottle again but this time I came to my senses before things got out of hand and I got myself into the flower shop on Broadway. That's where I met Phil. Three months later we were married. He was the first person I ever met who let me do the talking and, boy, did I have a lot to say. All that stuff bottled up inside me and Phil listened until I got rid of it all. I felt like a swimmer coming up for air.'

She took a deep breath and closed her eyes. 'Hey, I shouldn't be bothering you with all this old malarkey. You've had enough trouble for one night.'

'It's alright,' Nora said, 'I think I know how you feel.'

It seemed to Nora that Fay had talked enough. Reliving all the pain of her past was simply causing her more hurt and anguish. When Nora got into bad humour herself she often did the same thing and sometimes it took whole days for the misery to go away.

'Maybe you should go to bed,' Nora said. 'You look very tired.'

'I want to tell you about Phil,' Fay insisted, 'You haven't seen what he's really like. I want you to know he's a good man, a wonderful man....'

'There's no need to,' Nora pleaded but Fay had already begun.

'When I met Phil he was making big money. We had this enormous apartment. Well, enormous compared to this,' she smiled, looking around the sitting room that seemed smaller than ever in the half-light. 'He was working on a tunnel under the Hudson River with this bunch of Irish guys. I never even thought of the danger until one day he came home shaking from head to toe and white as a ghost. Seems the tunnel got flooded and five of his pals drowned. He was lucky to escape but he wasn't the same for a long time. In the end, we talked it all out and decided it was best for him to quit even if it meant moving out of that swell place. He got the job at the bank then and started going to night classes, drawing and painting. Got time to read. You know it's all he really wants, art and those poetry books but he just doesn't have time anymore, not since he took out the loan.'

Nora bristled on hearing this. It seemed that Fay was again blaming the boys for her latest misfortune.

'Don't get me wrong now, Nora,' Fay declared, 'There was always something missing from our lives when we didn't have kids. It's OK for some but when you want them real bad, it eats into you. See, the bottom line is me and Phil can't have our own kids. Maybe I need the guys too much. Maybe I turned a blind eye to Denis 'cause I knew deep down he was goin' haywire and I didn't want to admit I was a lousy mother.'

The revelations were coming too thick and fast for Nora to keep up with them. Her hand ached with a poisonous gnawing as if to punish her for her unthinking attacks on Fay.

'I'm sorry for all those things I said to you,' she said.

'Don't be crazy. There's nothing to be sorry for.'

'But there is.'

'Let me tell you how I see it,' Fay said. 'When the guys came over here I guess I had to take your mother's place but it wasn't as simple as that. I had to take your place too. If someone tried to take my place I reckon I'd want to kick their butts too.'

Nora laughed out loud. Fay's sense of humour was never far from the surface even when she was at her most serious. Nora liked that. It seemed to her the only way to survive the odds stacked against you.

'But really,' she insisted, 'all that nonsense about your clothes and all. I suppose it was just jealousy.'

It was strange to be making such admissions but Fay had revealed so much of herself so readily that it was somehow natural for Nora to do the same.

'I know all about jealousy, Nora. When I was in that orphanage there was this real pretty young girl who used to visit with her father. See, it was his money that kept the place going. I used to think she was the most beautiful creature on this earth. But as the years went on and she got taller and more confident I began to hate her. For a long time after I'd left the place I thought I'd just been jealous of her good looks, her clothes, the way she walked. Then when all this stuff started pouring out for poor Phil to listen to, it came to me.

The real reason I was jealous. She had what I couldn't have and it wasn't beauty or style. It was something more important than that.'

The vision of a privileged young girl conjured up by these words was so like Nora's own first impression of Fay that she was quite startled. It was as if her own innermost thoughts were being laid bare. She wasn't sure if she liked the feeling.

'Much more important,' Fay declared, 'she had parents. A mother and father. Maybe that's how you felt about me. I had what you wanted most. Your brothers.'

Fay was right and Nora knew it, in her heart, in the bloating beneath her wound, in the catch at the back of her throat.

'But this is different, Nora, you gotta believe me,' her aunt told her. 'Denis and Ritchie will always be your brothers. They don't need to talk about you every day for me to know you're always on their minds. I can't even begin to describe the excitement here when we got word you were on your way. I take care of them and we hit it off real good but they've only got one sister and that's you, kid. And, hey, now that we've cleared the air between us there's something else I gotta say.'

Nora wasn't sure if she could take any more, so choked was she with emotion. However, the glint of Fay's smile held the promise of some light relief.

'About the kitchen,' Fay said. 'And the electricity and all those gadgets that take the elbow-grease out of work.'

Where this was leading Nora had no notion but she was curious and glad of the chance to regain her composure.

'You and me, we got at least one thing in common....'

'More than one,' Nora said.

'I guess so. But we're both women and who ends up in the kitchen and cleaning the house? Sure, sometimes we get a little help but it's always down to us in the end. Electricity is the best thing that ever happened to us women. Why do you think it took so long for us to get up off our sweet little bottoms and start shouting for our rights? Too busy in the kitchen, that's why.'

Nora wondered what Molly would think of all this talk. She couldn't imagine her changing her old ways. The loading of the kitchen range with fuel, boiling water slowly on the hob, laboriously spinning the butter-maker. Yet, even though she did these things, who was Nora to say that she wouldn't appreciate the benefits of electricity especially if blindness overwhelmed her.

Nora could only be sure of her own feelings on the matter. Now that her eyes had been opened to the possibilities she knew that she could never go back to thinking that the old ways were best. She had every intention of leading an independent life and following her musical career. Anything that would allow more time to concentrate on that had to be good.

But would there be a musical career for her now? She slipped back the bandage and peered at the wound. There didn't appear to be any swelling nor any other explanation for the fierce, pulsating sensation in her palm. She wasn't reassured. Whatever invisible, sinister thing lay among the tissues of her hand was, she was certain, spreading its filthy tentacles in a network of evil intent. Yes, the fingers moved at will now and they looked fine if a little bloodless. However, each movement of them reminded her of the last, convulsive kicks of a dying insect.

She folded her arms close so she wouldn't have to look at her hands. So absorbed had she become in her own repulsive thoughts that she had forgotten altogether about Fay. They'd come so close that she felt bad about suddenly becoming so distant.

However, Fay too was lost in her own thoughts and didn't seem offended by Nora's silence. The clock on the wall struck three and fully ten minutes passed by before Fay spoke again.

'If only we could get away to the Midwest,' she said, 'It would be so good. See, this guy Phil met at the art classes, he's set up a small advertising business out there and he's offered Phil a job as an illustrator. He'd be so happy there, doing something he really loves.'

She stood up suddenly and went to the closet door. As usual, some boxes tumbled out but she took no notice. After some searching she drew out a large cardboard folder. She pointed at the framed pictures on the wall and declared, 'This stuff he's hung up, it's just some early stuff. Let me show you how good he really is.'

She laid the folder out on the table and opened it. Inside were dozens of sheets of all sizes covered with sketches and paintings. As Fay flicked each one over, Nora could see Phil's talent develop before her very eyes. At the beginning were several more sketches of buildings like those on the wall, perfectly drawn but somehow lifeless.

Soon, however, she noticed the drawings become livelier, the buildings less obviously drawn with a ruler, less perfectly square or rectangular, more lived in. There followed coloured landscapes. The burnished autumnal hues of trees, the distant haze of green-grey mountains, the blue-white spray of sea shores. With each one, it seemed he had learned some new trick that lent the feel of reality while capturing the magic of the ordinary.

Towards the end of the bundle, sketches of faces began to emerge, becoming more and more lifelike. Alongside many of them were the photographs and newspaper clippings he'd based the drawings on. Here was the US President, Calvin Coolidge; the actor, Rudolf Valentino; Mary Pickford, the actress Nora so admired, and other faces less familiar to her. Fay turned over another page and Nora was astonished to find herself staring at another all-too-familiar face.

Right there before her, his left eye almost appearing to twitch, was the mysterious stranger who had taken such an interest in her on board the SS *Bremen*. Alongside was the rough face of the man who'd come to her rescue earlier that day. The same man, she was now convinced, who'd saved her from being knocked down as she crossed the street to the First Mutual Bank.

'Who's this?' Nora asked, trying to disguise the sense of urgency she suddenly felt.

'Not a nice guy, Nora, I can tell you,' Fay said with a shiver. 'Corelli. Vincent Corelli. The other one's his sidekick. They call him The Fist. He used to be a boxer. The Fist Mantini.'

'They're gangsters?'

'Yeah, you could say that. Some people say he's been trying to go straight. He's been trying to cover his tracks, putting his money into big oil companies and stuff like that but now the income tax people are after him and he's in deep trouble. They say if he don't get shot by some other hoodlum he'll end up in jail anyway.'

'Is he a friend of Lefty Feeney and Harry Ruby?' Nora wondered.

'God, no. See, there's four, maybe five big-time hoodlums in this city. Dutch Schultz, Rothstein, Waxey Gordon, Vincent Corelli. This guy Ruby's another one of them and, see, they're like a little family. The kind that never talks to each other, except to argue. Some of them grew up together and started out in the same street gangs. Now they hate each other and Corelli and Ruby hate each other more than most. Something about a woman, the rumour goes. The bottom line is these gangsters got the city divided up between them and they get rich on running booze and gambling rackets, fixing fights, whatever it takes for the fast buck.'

At first it had seemed incredible that she should have been befriended by Corelli while Phil and Denis were, at the same time, being blackmailed by Ruby, his arch-enemy. Soon, however, it didn't seem such a coincidence. After all, there were so few 'brothers' in this 'family' of gangsters and between them they touched the lives of tens, perhaps hundreds of thousands of innocent citizens.

'I've gone and worn you out now, haven't I?' Fay said. 'I'd better make myself scarce before I start talking again.'

'I'm glad you told me all this.'

'And I'm grateful that you listened. If I could only do something for you.'

Late as it was, Nora sat on the narrow couch for a long time trying to put the pieces of these last few days together. It was clear that this fellow they called The Fist was following her on Corelli's orders. But the question was why? And how had Corelli known she was in trouble? Was it Corelli's men too who'd come to Phil's assistance when he was being beaten up? No matter how hard she tried she couldn't make sense of the whole business.

However, the only question that mattered now was whether she should contact Corelli. The voices in her head, one telling her that her hand was alright, the other that there was something very dangerous happening there, were no help in her efforts to decide.

This bandaged hand was, it seemed to her, the only means of gaining Corelli's sympathy. If he discovered there was nothing really wrong with it, how would he react? Would he think she had tried to trick him into helping her brothers?

All through the night she failed to cross the threshold of sleep. Then, in the early hours of the morning, a hushed argument in the kitchen forced her into a decision.

CHAPTER 15

Nora edged awkwardly from her couch and moved silently towards the kitchen door which was slightly ajar. She heard Fay's voice rise suddenly and just as quickly descend to a heated whisper. Phil's tone was deeper, more insistent. Pressing herself against the wall and breathing in and out shallowly, she listened.

'I have to go,' Phil was saying.

'But you know what the doctor said,' Fay muttered.

'I feel fine, honestly.'

'Just take a look in the mirror, Phil. You look awful.'

'I got to go back to work.'

'Why, Phil? What difference will a few days make? I can get some extra hours at the shop to make up for it.'

'I have to go,' Phil repeated, 'I can't tell you why. It's better you don't know.'

'Don't treat me like that. I won't take it, d'ye hear me? I won't have secrets between us.'

A sense of panic overcame Nora as a momentary silence fell on the kitchen. She was sure one or other of them was about to come to the door and discover her there. Inching away, she was stopped in her tracks when Phil began to speak again. She had to strain every sinew to hear his words.

'If I don't go in today,' he said, 'I won't be able to do this job for Lefty Feeney and what choice do I have now? I've got to get Denis out of this fix. And now there's Nora to think of. I can't let her home without having her hand checked out properly.'

Fay paused before she answered as if, like Nora outside, she was tumbling slowly to the truth.

'You're going to help Feeney rob the bank, am I right?'

There was no reply.

'Am I right?' Fay hissed angrily.

'I won't be involved...not really...I've just got to give him the low-down on this big cash delivery that's coming in...the time and place...that kind of thing. Fay, you know the kind of guy I am, I wouldn't do this unless I had to.'

'Maybe I just *thought* I knew the kind of guy you were.'

'Don't say that, Fay, please. Remember that first time they broke my ribs, well, it wasn't because of the loan. See, they wanted me to give them a tip-off on another lodgement just like this one but I wouldn't do it. Then they came and told me about Denis and Ryan's store. I had to agree to help them with a job they'd planned for the week after Nora went home...or the week after I thought she was going home. When I told them they'd have to wait until Nora was gone they beat me up again. Now they want to go ahead tomorrow. They got word of a big deposit. If I don't show up they're gonna kill me, Fay.'

'How much money is there?' Fay asked very softly.

'A million dollars,' Phil told her. 'There's twenty thousand in it for us.'

'For us,' Fay exclaimed, 'Do you really think I'd touch a nickel of it?'

'Look, we'll just take what we need for Nora's treatment and our fare to the Midwest, that's all.'

'We're never gonna make it to Dennsville now, are we?' Fay said despairingly.

'Sure we are,' he said, sounding unconvinced.

A chair scraped back along the kitchen floor and Nora dashed quickly behind the curtain where her couch lay. She heard Phil's careful tread across the sitting room floor and the apartment door closed out with a quiet, but dreadful, finality. At that very moment she made up her mind to go to Corelli.

In many ways, the chance she was about to take was an outrageous one. Her real purpose would be to ask for his help in saving Phil and the family from the clutches of Feeney and Ruby. To do that, however, she would have to get on the right side of this gangster. Only one way came to mind. She would have to promise to take up the offer of going to the Foundation if he paid for her hand to be fixed up. The chance was an outrageous one because, firstly, there was no guarantee she'd even be offered a place at the Foundation. Was he likely even to believe, any more than the doctor had, that her concern was justified?

She had no reason in the world to think her plan would work, only a vague feeling that despite his reputation Corelli might have some humanity in him. She forced to the back of her mind all thoughts of Peter and Molly and how she would tell them she was going to stay in New York, concentrating instead on the more immediate problems ahead.

First there was the question of how she would meet Corelli. She had no idea of where he lived and she couldn't very well ask Fay. The answer came to her in a flash. She knew she was being followed everywhere by The Fist. Therefore, it was simply a matter of going out into the streets and waiting for him to appear. She would confront him and ask to be taken to Corelli.

The next problem was to find some excuse to be out of the apartment for however long it took to meet Corelli. She didn't want to simply disappear. Now that she knew Fay better she felt she couldn't add to her worries. She decided to write a note that didn't, no matter how hard she struggled, sound very convincing: *Dear Fay, I'm going out to buy some presents for my friends at home. I didn't like to wake you but I'll be back at lunchtime, Nora.*

She heard Fay go back into her bedroom and began to dress. It proved to be a harrowing task. Her bandaged hand was as rigid as if sculpted from stone. She wondered if her mind was playing tricks with her, trying to fool her into believing that paralysis had set in. Minutes before she had been trying to read Corelli's mind. Now she realised she couldn't even understand her own.

All the way along Wash-Basin Street she thought about the ridiculous excuse she'd made in her note and several times was on the point of turning back. The heat of the day was beginning to rise from the pavement and press down from the cloudless sky. The air was already too thick to breathe.

Turning into the next street she pretended to take a great interest in the shop windows. The truth was she was searching there for a reflection of the big broken-nosed boxer among the passersby hurrying to work. If he was nearby he was hiding himself well. As she wandered slowly on the fear rose in her that on this one day when she wanted to be followed, her pursuer wouldn't show up. Was it perhaps too early in the morning for him? More disconcerting still was the thought that perhaps Corelli had already given up on her.

But it was another, altogether different thought that suddenly made her stop dawdling and hurry away as far as possible from Wash-Basin Street. What if, instead of The Fist, Danny Feeney's contemptible little face showed up in the shop windows?

Her pace slowed again as she found herself drifting into streets that were more and more crowded. As tempting as it was to look back over her shoulder she willed herself not to. The chances were that this would merely scare The Fist off.

She had walked so far by now that she knew she wouldn't

be able to find her way back. Worse still, she had forgotten to bring any of the few dollars Peter had given her for her holiday. Up ahead she saw Macy's, a monumental, multi-storeyed shop and decided to go inside. If The Fist was really following her she might have a better chance of spotting him in there.

The air was cool in the broad expanses of the store. At each counter she made a great show of examining every item. As preoccupied as she was she couldn't help but wonder at the extravagance and expense of the clothes and hats and jewellery on display. Here was a silk dress for fifteen dollars. More than a month's pay back in Ireland. More surprising still was the fact that so many people could afford the prices. Cash registers rang all around with the shallow music of coins.

'Much wants more,' she heard Aunt Molly whisper as if she was there alongside her, and she had to smile.

At the hat stand she touched soft leather and felts and satins shaped into an abundance of styles, most of them more than curious. The price tags astounded her. She tried on a black felt one that fitted neatly on to the back of her head. From its side there hung down a sweep of green netting and when she looked in the mirror on the counter she almost laughed out loud. It was so ridiculous that she wondered whether she had it on the right way at all. She moved it around with her good hand until the netting fell over her eyes. Then through a green haze she saw the face she'd been searching for. Her heart beat fast but she took the hat slowly from her head and walked on.

She approached a wide column with a mirror on its lower end. In the reflection she could see he was still in pursuit. She stepped deftly behind the column and The Fist passed hurriedly by. Now, he was the one being followed. He dashed from one counter to the next, knocking clumsily against outraged shoppers. She seemed to be able to anticipate his every turn so that each time he swung around she was out of sight.

Finally, he stood defeated beside a perfume counter. A salesgirl tidying up the shelves regarded him with suspicion. Nora stole up behind him and when she got within a few feet she called out, 'Are you looking for me, by any chance?'

He wheeled around quickly, glanced and lowered his eyes. His face was deeply creased and nut-hard, the nose flat and boneless.

'No,' he blustered.

She could almost hear his mind ticking over, searching for an excuse. He looked up at the ranks of perfume bottles.

'I been getting some scent for a lady friend,' he hissed, 'Now scram, kid, and stop bothering me.'

'I know who you are and who you work for.'

'You do?'

'They call you The Fist and you're Corelli's henchman.'

'I ain't no henchman,' he objected, 'I'm an assistant.'

'Well, whatever you call yourself,' Nora said, 'I need to see Mr Corelli.'

He looked at her doubtfully. His eyes searched the store and finally came to rest on her bandaged hand.

'What's with the mitt, kid?' he asked in a hushed voice.

'Mitt?'

'Your hand, kid,' he said, offended that she hadn't understood him, 'D'ye hurt it or what?'

'Yes, and I need to have it seen to or...' Nora started and playing for his sympathy squeezed out a tear.

'Didn't you see a doctor?'

Nora couldn't answer. The pretence of pain and loss had become real and wouldn't allow words. Though the man's glare had begun to melt into sympathy, her misery wasn't relieved. The certainty that no specialist, no matter how expensive, could save her hand was too overwhelming. She had to remind herself that she was only going through with this plan for the sake of her brothers and her aunt and uncle.

'Come on, kid, the Boss'll take care of that. Don't you go worrying now.'

She followed him out of the store, embarrassed by his very obvious display of care and attention.

'Let me get the door for you. Watch the step now. Hey, buddy, can't you see the kid's hurt bad? Watch where you're walking, you dummy. Cab! Hey, over here, baloney head. I got a emergency.'

It was with the greatest relief that she climbed into the taxi-cab, even though it felt like the inside of an oven in there. More awful still was the faint smell of baby-sick that clung to the very leather of the seat. She sank back and closed her eyes.

'Holy smoke, she's out cold,' The Fist yelled, 'Open a window or I'll knock your block off. Don't you ever clean this pigsty?'

Nora, however, was simply trying to sort out in her mind what she'd say to Corelli. She opened her eyes briefly to put the big man out of his misery.

'I'm grand,' she told him, 'There's no need to be roaring like a jackass.'

He folded his arms and glared straight ahead. It was difficult to believe that this bumbling fellow was capable of any crime. Still, she thought Corelli was faintly ridiculous too until he'd lost his temper. And Fay had left her in no doubt as to what these men were really like.

If she imagined it was to some hellish, smoke-filled hovel she was being taken, she couldn't have been more wrong. They left the city behind them and passed through suburbs lined with mansion after mansion. As they went along, each one seemed larger and had longer and more widely-curving driveways. On their left there loomed a high wall that stretched for fully half a mile. Eventually they came to a set of gates and The Fist stuck his head out the window of the cab and yelled something Nora couldn't quite catch.

Out of nowhere, two men with sub-machine-guns came and swung the gates open. As they passed through the grand gate pillars she caught a glimpse of a brass name-plate. 'Villa Dolorosa', it declared. 'Dolorosa'. The word rang in her head as they swept along the winding road to a vast yellow house, gleaming under the late morning sun. 'Dolorosa'. She knew it was familiar, something she'd heard at school. 'Dolorosa'. The taxi came to a crunching halt, dwarfed by the massive edifice of the house and then it came to her. 'Dolorosa' was the Latin word for 'sadness', and 'Villa'? That was easy, it meant 'house'.

Why would anyone put such a name on their gate for all the world to see? Nora dragged herself up the broad steps after The Fist. The front door opened and he disappeared inside.

On the threshold she stood listening to his voice in the echoing cavern of the 'Villa Dolorosa', 'The House of Sadness'.

CHAPTER 16

The dark greens and indifferent shades of grey inside bled the incoming light of all life. There was an absence of human warmth and no feeling about the place of being lived in. Or, at least, not of being lived in with any joy.

Somewhere above Nora a loud but indistinct argument started up. There followed the sound of men running and then from the heights came a piercing yell. It sounded like her own name but she couldn't be sure.

Corelli descended the dark staircase, his face contorted with that look of withering menace she'd seen once before. She couldn't help but feel his anger was directed at her. He stopped suddenly at the foot of the stairs, his crazed eyes settling on her bandaged hand. Behind him, The Fist trundled down the steps sheepishly. His tie had been loosened and his hair stood up as if it had been pulled and tossed about.

'It ain't my fault, Boss,' he grumbled, 'Tell him, will you kid?'

'Mr Corelli, I asked your friend to bring me here. It wasn't his idea.'

'I ain't worried about you coming here,' he fumed, 'I want to know what happened your hand when this dummy was supposed to be tailing you. Who did it? Feeney? Ruby? I'll make them pay, nothing surer. I'll throw them in the Hudson with a concrete lifejacket.'

'It was an accident, Mr Corelli,' Nora lied, 'I cut it with a steak knife in the apartment.'

'How bad is it?'

'The doctor says there's nothing to worry about but I have this feeling...like there's something in there that shouldn't be...I'm sorry, I can't explain it...it just feels...bad.'

His madly twitching eye was almost hypnotic. She couldn't escape its dizzying contortions.

'If I could see someone,' she said as if speaking in a trance, 'someone who knows what he's doing. The doctor mentioned a Mr Stoneleigh at the...the Brim...Brimstead Private Clinic but it would cost an awful lot.'

'You got it, kid,' Corelli said, 'Always trust your own instincts, that's what I say. Get this guy on the phone, Fist.'

Nora came quickly to her senses. How could it be this simple? In the fierce glow of his concern she forgot for the moment all she knew about him. She had expected to have to bargain to get even this far with him. Instead, he had agreed to have her hand seen to without question.

'I really don't know if it's that bad,' she blurted out, 'Maybe you shouldn't waste your money.'

'I'd sell this dump if I had to just to be sure, kid.'

'But it could be a beautiful house if you only brightened it up.'

'It's a garbage can.' He sniffed and had no more to say on the subject.

Just then The Fist bellowed out from a room nearby.

'Stoneleigh says he's all booked up for a month, Boss. You want me to come the heavy on him?'

'Keep him on the line,' Corelli shouted and brought Nora to a plush seat near the stairway. 'You just take a rest now, kid, I'll talk to this guy, see what I can do.'

He spoke with the confident air of a man who always got what he wanted. Striding away purposefully he elbowed open the door of the room where The Fist was still talking to Stoneleigh. The big man emerged and closed the door quietly after him. He walked up and down like a guard on duty. Catching Nora's eye he winked foolishly and grinned.

'This Stoneleigh guy, he'll see you in double-quick time.'

Corelli's voice rose and fell for a minute or two until finally Nora heard the telephone being slammed back in its cradle. When he appeared at the door his face had taken on an impatient scowl. He gestured at The Fist to follow him and headed for the front door.

'Come on, kid,' he called to Nora and rounding on The Fist yelled, 'Go and help her, you dumb palooka.'

Nora wondered why a tough man like The Fist would take this treatment from someone half his size. It seemed to her that fear could be the only reason. The same reason, she supposed, that this Mr Stoneleigh had agreed to see her. And why did she seem to be the only person he showed any human feeling for?

As the luxurious green and white convertible sped towards Long Island she tried to imagine Corelli's reaction if the treatment was unsuccessful. It wasn't likely to be one of polite acceptance.

'Mr Corelli,' she asked, 'If he can't do anything for me, you won't take it out on him, will you?'

'You pay top dollars,' he said flatly, 'you expect results.'

'Don't hurt him, please.'

'Sure,' he said, 'but we ain't gonna think negative, kid. You're gonna be playing them keyboards in no time.'

At the Brimstead Private Clinic, a low white building surrounded by exotic gardens, Corelli swept through the busy corridors and called out to a blue-coated janitor, 'Where's this Stoneleigh guy hang out?'

'Fourth door on the right,' the janitor said with a shrug, 'But let me give you a tip, go get yourself an appointment first. He don't see nobody without an appointment.'

Corelli shot him a dark look.

'And I got a tip for you, dummy.'

'Yeah?' the man sneered.

'Nobody gives Vincent Corelli no tip.'

The janitor dropped his broom and backed away. They reached the door with its neat little name-plate announcing 'Mr Raymond G. Stoneleigh', followed by a string of mysterious abbreviations.

'What's all the letters mean after the punk's name, Boss?' The Fist asked.

'They mean dough. For every letter you pay another hundred dollars. How long did it take getting here?'

'Sixteen minutes, Boss.'

'Good, we're early,' Corelli rasped, 'Maybe we'll get a discount.'

Something in his cynical smile told Nora Stoneleigh would be lucky to be paid at all. Corelli opened the door on an expensively decorated waiting room. There were three people sitting there in various states of anxiety. So concerned were they with their own problems that they barely glanced at the intruders.

At a desk beside a further door sat a young secretary who didn't look very happy to see them. She was rustling through a folder of documents and trying very hard to appear calm.

'Name, please,' she asked without looking up.

'Just tell the doc, Corelli's here, OK?' he ordered, moving his face within inches of hers.

'He's got a patient in there right now.'

'Tell him!' Corelli snapped.

The telephone shook in the secretary's hand. After a very few hesitant words and a distant crackling answer from the other end, the young woman cranked her face into a broken smile.

'Just a moment...sir,' she said, 'He'll be with...'

Suddenly the door beside her burst open to reveal a flushed and fuming old woman. She brushed past Corelli, her fussy bulk sending him rocking back unsteadily on his heels.

'The Medical Board will hear about this,' she shouted, 'I will not be dealt with in this perfunctory manner.'

The trembling secretary walked her to the waiting room door.

'You'd like to make a further appointment, madame?' she asked of the fur-coated lady.

'Certainly not,' the woman announced and stormed out.

The other patients moved about uneasily in their seats. Nora could see that they too had now recognised Corelli, whose picture often appeared on the city's newspapers. She felt suddenly ashamed to be in his company and wished she could tell these people just why she was with him.

A tall, lean man now stood at the door from which the old woman had emerged moments before. At the end of his long, pointed noise a pair of spectacles was finely balanced. He stared sullenly out over them.

'If you'd like to come this way,' he mumbled, gritting his teeth.

Corelli told The Fist to stay in the waiting room and he and Nora followed the doctor inside. Seated behind his desk, the doctor pointed to the chairs where they should sit. Nora took her place quietly but Corelli sat on the desk.

'You've got a problem, then?' the doctor began.

'It's your problem now, doc,' Corelli said with a sly grin.

'Yes,' the doctor laughed weakly, 'I suppose you could say that.'

'My friend here,' Corelli explained, 'she's a piano-player — a pianist — and she's had an accident with her hand. Some horse-doctor says it's OK but she ain't sure.'

Stoneleigh left the comfort of his seat and came around the

desk. As he passed by Corelli his shoulders flinched. He began to remove the bandage with the greatest of care.

'Perhaps you'd like to wait outside, Mr Corelli?' he suggested with some trepidation.

'Hey, I'll be quiet as a mouse.'

Nora knew the doctor would be too nervous to concentrate properly with Corelli standing over him. Whatever chance she had, she needed Stoneleigh's full attention.

'Please?' Nora asked of Corelli.

He seemed a little offended but soon softened again.

'Sure,' he agreed uncertainly, 'I guess I'm in the way. I don't think I really want to see this anyway. These things upset me. Blood and grizzle, you know.'

Stoneleigh looked at Nora. It wasn't difficult to guess what he was thinking. Corelli left and, at last, the bandage was unrolled.

'Good God,' Stoneleigh gasped, 'Who stitched this up?'

'I don't know his name. Some doctor on Wash-Basin Street.'

'You're friend was right about one thing,' he said, 'This *is* the work of a horse-doctor.'

Before she had a chance to say that Corelli wasn't what you'd call a friend exactly, Stoneleigh had gone to fetch a glittering box of medical implements.

'I don't know what this fellow was thinking of stitching it up in the first place. He's pulled it so tight you'd find yourself left with a bunch of crab claws.'

There was a certain relief, however shortlived, in knowing her doubts hadn't been misplaced.

'I'm afraid this is going to hurt.'

As soon as the cold metal of the forceps touched the raw edges of her wound the pain began its manic darting, shooting out into her fingers, along the underside of her arm to her elbow and on and on until it seemed her whole body was possessed by it. Aware of Corelli's presence in the next room she couldn't scream. Instead, she hummed softly. But the agonised melody Stoneleigh heard was a mere echo of the mad, thundering cavalcade of raw music, battering the pain in her brain into submission.

The stitches removed,s he cleansed the wound of the yellow ooze that soon began to seep through.

'Maybe you'd better start singing again,' he advised her as he drew the torn folds of skin apart and delved beneath with yet another instrument of torture.

She groaned a low note. D, she told herself, No. D flat. And her agony rose to a whisper beyond the far reaches of any keyboard to an impossible B sharp, was it? Then down the scales again she whimpered, down to a middle C and below to the end, to the last, the first bass note, the sombre A.

All the while, the devilish milk of infection flowed and it seemed her insides were made up entirely of this putrid puss. Stoneleigh talked to himself continuously as he worked and his spectacles steamed up with the heat of concentration and effort.

'Damn fool,' he muttered and for some strange reason Nora felt pity for that other clumsy doctor on Wash-Basin Street.

'I'm sure he did his best,' she said, forgetting the misery he'd put her through.

'All I can say is, his best wasn't good enough. Not by a long shot. You might have lost this hand, do you realise that? I can't even say for sure yet if...'

Her concern had all been about not being able to use her hand. The possibility of losing it altogether hadn't entered her mind. The shock of his uncertainty had a peculiar effect. Her hand went numb. She felt nothing of the probing instrument now.

At first, the absence of feeling was terrifying but slowly a soothing sense of utter detachment overcame her. It was extraordinary, it was wrong-headed of her but she didn't care what happened next.

My hand, she had to remind herself, that strange wriggling thing is my hand. For indeed it was moving though she felt not a thing, not even Stoneleigh's heavy breath, his head lowered within inches of the wound. It was so good not to have to endure the pain anymore that she drifted away altogether.

She saw Stoneleigh as if from a great distance, working on her hand and realised that for all his efforts it was down to her now. She could let this infection invade her completely and remove her altogether from being into nothingness. Or she could defy it and defy every other obstacle to fulfilment.

Which way should I choose? she asked herself casually. And the answer wasn't made of words. It was a tune, a childish tinkering among the bright ivories and dark ebonies of a piano. And with it came a memory.

Mrs Teehan's parlour. Nora seated at the piano. Her mother and Mrs Teehan stand, one by each shoulder. Denis and Ritchie, their heads barely reaching to the keyboard, stand to her left and to her right. Their small hands reach tremulously upwards and touch out a delighted, clattering bass and melody.

All at once she knew she must have her hand back. Music was what kept her body and soul together. It was the key to that eternity where all those she had ever loved waited to live again. And live again they would, in the music she made.

Her hand began to tremble beneath the gentle prodding of Stoneleigh's silver forceps. Her fingers curled into a fist. For a moment, she thought she was merely grasping at a sliver of light. Then came the delicious coldness, the harsh, solid touch of reality.

'I can feel it.'

His disapproving look didn't bother her. She opened out

her hand and offered him his forceps just as music had offered her back the will to live.

When Stoneleigh had finished his poking about and his dabbing on of ointment all she was left with was a harmlessly itchy sensation in her palm.

'I think I've cleared it,' he said, wiping his brow. 'Another few days and I'd have had to amputate. I found some gangrene but I believe we're over the worst.'

Nora wasn't surprised at this news. She knew how close she'd come to the brink of disaster.

'You'll need to come here every day for maybe a week so's I can dress the wound,' he told her.

'That's alright.'

'Look, I don't seem to have made myself clear,' he indicated, surprised by her indifference. 'The risk of infection hasn't passed and I still can't guarantee you'll have a full reach with that hand.'

'I know.' His misgivings meant nothing to her so certain was she that her fighting spirit would lead to a complete healing. He eyed her curiously over his spectacles, unsure what to make of this remarkably unruffled young girl.

'What was that tune you were humming?' he asked.

'I don't know. Nobody's written it yet, I suppose.'

'Maybe you'll write it yourself then.'

'Yes. I'll call it *Mr Stoneleigh's Serenade*.'

He swept off his glasses and stood up, letting out a quiet, unexpectedly hearty laugh.

'That would be an honour indeed, young lady.'

The door behind her burst open and she turned to see Corelli fix a questioning gaze on Stoneleigh.

'You guys wanna share the joke?' he said, like a child asking for his slice of cake.

'Miss Canavan has offered to put my name on her new composition,' Stoneleigh announced trying desperately to hold on to his unnatural smile.

'Oh, right.'

Corelli seemed uncomfortable, no longer in command.

'So what's the score?' he asked brusquely.

He listened in growing confusion to the welter of medical terms. Talk of 'prognosis', the onset of 'septicaemia', 'muscular atrophy'. Nora wondered if Stoneleigh was wise in testing Corelli's patience like this. However, she was surprised to see Corelli sit down quietly and stare at the floor until the lecturer had ended.

'It's looking good then, I take it,' he contended and it seemed as though he'd had to make a great effort to return from wherever his thoughts had wandered.

'Time will tell,' Stoneleigh answered weakly, 'but I guess we should know pretty well when she comes tomorrow.'

Drawing a veil over his remaining doubts he went on to explain how he would dress the wound regularly through the next week, how Nora would get the best of care and how his clinic was renowned for getting the best results in the most perilous of situations. Corelli didn't show whether or not he was convinced.

'I guess we can talk about money tomorrow then,' he said as he and Nora prepared to leave.

Stoneleigh wasn't happy but he wasn't about to say so.

'Sure, it can wait.'

Outside, in the wide spaces of the clinic's gardens, the heat wasn't as oppressive as it was in the heart of the city. That Midwest she hoped the boys would soon reach might be just like this. In spite of the heavy-heartedness this thought brought with it, she thanked Corelli. She still had another favour to ask of him and until she brought herself to do that, she would have to charm him with her politeness.

'You don't have to thank me,' he said, 'and listen, don't call me Mister. Call me Vincent, OK?'

The journey back to the city was less frenetic and there was time for Nora and Corelli to talk. In truth, it was Corelli who did most of the talking. As she listened she discovered why she was so favoured by this man who had nothing but contempt for just about everybody else.

The reason for his interest in Nora, he admitted, wasn't altogether because of her talent, though he was more than impressed by it. Nora, he explained, reminded him of his own daughter, Maria, who once played the piano too. Encouraged by his wife, Oriana, Maria had attended the LaFonde Musical Foundation. Though not quite as gifted as Nora, she had been doing very well.

At the same time, Oriana was convincing Corelli to leave his criminal past behind. He began to invest his money in companies that were strictly legal. However, his sworn enemy, Harry Ruby, didn't like what was happening. He was afraid that Corelli would pass on the many secrets he knew about him to the police. Corelli had no intention of doing this but Ruby chose to believe he would.

Ruby organised a gang to attack and kill Corelli. He discovered that Corelli and his wife were to attend a symphony in downtown New York. As they got into their car afterwards, Ruby's men pounced and opened up with eight submachine guns.

Corelli choked on his words as he struggled to get them out. Nora listened with growing astonishment as the facts became clear to her. Three of Corelli's men lay dead on the pavement after the attack. His wife, Oriana, died on the way to hospital.

'That filthy punk Ruby had the nerve to send me a message. Claimed they hadn't set out to kill her and he was calling off his goons if I didn't come after him. The crazy thing was, Oriana was his girlfriend before I snatched her from him. We was good friends, me and Ruby, but when she married me, he took it real bad. I didn't give him no answer but I didn't start no gang war neither. I guess I didn't have the heart for it. Not after Maria turned on me.'

Maria, who was eighteen then, blamed Corelli for her mother's death. She refused to speak to him ever again and finally left for Europe, where she still lived. He had no idea where she was exactly although he'd hired private detectives in every European country to trace her. When he'd met Nora on board the SS *Bremen* he was returning from Berlin where a girl had been located who fitted her description precisely. He'd found a young American girl alright but it wasn't Maria.

'Sometimes,' he told Nora, 'I'm not sure if I really want to find her. I wouldn't know what to say.'

'I'm sure you'd think of something,' Nora maintained but it was easy to understand Maria's wish to have nothing to do with him.

'It ain't gonna happen anyways. You know, for years I been convincing myself that everything I done was for her sake and Oriana's. So's they could have whatever they wanted and not have to live in a slum like I used to. But when Oriana died and Maria left I knew it was all a lie. I was doing it for myself. I wanted to be the top dog and maybe that's what I was — but it don't feel no good anymore.'

'Is that why you call your house, "Villa Dolorosa"?'

'I guess so,' he said and smiled briefly as he remembered. 'We moved into that place on Maria's tenth birthday. I paid over the top so's everything would be ready on time. She was so happy. See, we called it "Villa Maria". She was down at that gate every five minutes staring up at her name on the brass plate.'

Silence descended on the car as they re-entered the broiling heat of the city. The Fist tried to whistle nonchalantly, pretending he'd heard nothing of what Corelli had said.

'Why did you have me followed?' Nora asked.

'Hey, I'm sorry about that,' Corelli said, suddenly embarrassed. 'I guess I wanted to see if you'd take up my offer. That day you went to the Foundation, I felt my luck was really on the up. Then this Feeney guy sent some punk to hustle you so I had to find out why. You want to tell me about that?'

Her chance had come. Everything depended on how he would react to her story.

She told him about Phil's loan and about Denis and Danny Feeney and the 'Weebees'. How they robbed Ryan's store and how Lefty Feeney was now putting pressure on Phil to help out in robbing the bank. She went on to describe Phil's hope of moving to the Midwest and how Feeney and Ruby were standing in the way of this. Still unsure as to his true feelings she told him of her own difficult past, hoping that this would make him pity her even more.

He stared gravely out the cab window and she became ever more desperate. The truth about her cut hand spilled out like a last plea for sympathy. Corelli thought long and hard and finally told Nora what he was going to do.

'I can stop this bank job real fast,' he decided. 'Tomorrow, you say? Right, what I'll do is...I'll get the word to Ruby and Feeney that if they don't pull out of it and let your uncle off the hook, I'll tip off the bank.'

'But Ruby will come after you again if you do that,' Nora cried, realising she might be starting something that could end in a bloody battle between Corelli and Ruby.

'I got plenty of protection,' Corelli smiled, 'Am I right, Fist?'

'Ain't nobody gonna get near you, Boss,' The Fist declared, giving him the thumbs-up.

'I should never have asked you,' Nora said miserably.

Whether he was a gangster or not, he was a friend to her, confiding in her, willing to do anything for her. It was a strange admission to make even to herself but it was unavoidable.

'Don't you worry, kid,' he told her as they dropped her off at the junction of Wash-Basin Street. 'We'll send a taxi at nine in the morning. Be ready, OK?'

She offered her hand and he took it.

'Tell you're uncle from me to start packing,' he grinned.

Racing back to the apartment house she felt sure that Fay would quickly forgive her for disappearing when she heard the good news. Freedom was near for all of them. Except, perhaps, Nora herself.

But as she neared the apartment house, even this possibility didn't dismay her. If anything it left her all the more exhilarated. She would do anything for her brothers. Give up the comfort and security of her own home, live in this forbidding city, endure the cold depths of the LaFonde Foundation, enlist the aid of those society regarded as devils.

Love and loyalty, she'd always imagined, were the most innocent and decent of emotions. But when you crossed the dividing line between good and evil so readily to protect others, what became of innocence and what became of decency?

The door of the apartment house slammed shut behind her like a fist banging on a table, like a refusal to answer.

CHAPTER 17

'I had to go to Corelli,' Nora told Fay, 'because of...I'm sorry but I heard you and Phil talking before he left.'

The boys looked to Fay but she offered them no explanation.

'Last night I told you everything would work out fine,' Nora went on. 'And it has. The specialist says there's a good chance my hand will be alright. I just have to have it dressed regularly. And...'

Denis and Ritchie were overjoyed. The question of who was paying for the specialist never crossed their minds, as long as her hand was going to be healed. Fay, however, was obviously troubled though she put on a good show.

'That's wonderful, Nora,' she cried, 'Wonderful.'

'And there's something else, Fay,' Nora announced. 'That "job" Phil was talking about, at the bank, well it won't be happening now. Mr Corelli is dealing with it.'

Fay wanted to hear more but not in front of the boys.

'Guys, go and get Nora's dinner from the oven and set a place at the table for her.' They went reluctantly to the kitchen.

'And close the door,' Fay called.

The door slammed shut to a chorus of mumbles.

'Are you sure about this, Nora?'

'Of course I'm sure,' Nora said, angry with Fay for seeming so ungrateful.

'Sorry, Nora, it's just pretty hard for me to believe in good luck when it comes along, but if Corelli says the bank job is off, I guess they gotta listen.'

They heard footsteps on the stairs outside and Fay's head snapped towards the door. There was a fumbling of keys as she forced an unconvincing smile into play on her face. The door opened and Phil, his gaunt cheeks still badly bruised and showing the signs of his pain, walked in. He looked worried.

When Nora had gone through her story again for him he sat into his favourite chair but seemed ill-at-ease. His silence unnerved Nora.

'I don't like it,' he said finally.

'You don't like it?' Nora muttered.

'Look, I know you've done this with the best of intentions Nora, but it stinks. We're in it up to here with Ruby and Feeney. Now you've dragged Corelli into it, God knows where it will end.'

Nora looked to Fay for support but her aunt was clearly at a loss as to what to think.

'Do you have a better idea?' Nora asked.

He picked up one of his books from beside the chair as if he might find some answer there. Flicking through it carelessly, he drew in a deep breath and dropped the book on the floor at his feet.

'No, I don't,' he sighed, 'but I'm not taking Corelli's help. He doesn't do favours, Nora, not unless he's got some slimy reason.'

'I told you why he's helping us.'

'If you believe that old shoeshine, you'll believe anything. Didn't it ever occur to you he might just be using you to get at Ruby? That's his style, he's a user. All these people are. It's how they make a living.'

Phil's conclusion, as unwelcome as it was, had the ring of truth about it. She wanted to cry out, to tell him how much she was prepared to sacrifice for all of them. But if she did, he would be even more determined not to place their lives in Corelli's hands. What, she wondered, was she to do now? Let his obstinacy stop her from going back to the clinic and thereby risk losing her hand? Pass up the chance to free her brothers?

'Are you telling me to stay away from Corelli?' she asked him.

'I don't have the right to tell you what to do, just leave us out of it.'

'Us?'

'You know what I mean.'

'I'm to mind my own business, is it?' she murmured.

'He doesn't mean that,' Fay insisted.

'That's what it amounts to,' Nora said.

'I guess so,' Phil agreed.

'You can't accept that a man can change,' Nora said angrily, 'Even a man like Corelli. Your own brother, my father, he was a no-good drunkard and now he's...'

'Sure, a man can change,' Phil sighed, 'Look at me. I wasn't always a gutless bum.'

Fay went and knelt by his chair, grabbed his hands and squeezed them into fists. It was as if she was reminding him that he still had some strength left in him.

'I won't listen to this talk no more, Phil,' she said. 'You've tried. You've done everything one man could do. Maybe it's time to let someone help out. What's that line you used to have about loners, something about an island?'

'No man is an island, entire of itself.'

'Right. You can't always make out alone.'

'But Corelli. Of all people to turn to,' he complained. 'How can I live with that, knowing some hoodlum gave me back my future?'

The force of his quiet complaint rocked Nora. She too

would have to live with the knowledge that her musical future was tainted by its dependence on a criminal. Every time she touched the keys of a piano she would be haunted by this. She wondered how beauty or good could ever arise from the generosity of a man with Corelli's reputation.

It was frightening too that she'd never thought of this before. Or worse still that she'd hidden it from herself. It seemed to her that this was how evil people got by — avoiding all pangs of conscience. How easy it was to do.

Pulling Phil's hands towards her Fay peered into his troubled eyes.

'Seems to me you're already taking a big chance on Ruby and Feeney letting you off the hook if you help them. And maybe those stories about Corelli aiming to go straight are true. Maybe Nora is right about him. People *can* change. I did, remember?'

'Don't compare yourself to that gangster, Fay.'

'And why not? Who the hell is perfect? Get in too deep just once and the nicest person in the world can get sucked under. Even you, Phil, or me.'

Phil struggled painfully to his feet, shaking his head all the while.

'I'll have no part in it,' he muttered , as he left the room.

Fay waited for the bedroom door to close before she spoke. 'Do what you have to do, Nora. He knows there's no other way. He just can't make himself say it.'

~

Soon Nora found herself doubting even her own reason for going to Corelli. Could it be true that her brothers weren't after all her main concern? Was the threat to her musical career the real reason? Beneath the facade of sisterly devotion was there lurking some selfish, cold-hearted creature who would go to any length to reach her true goal?

The more she thought about the whole situation the more she realised she had fooled herself into a false sense of optimism. In the cruel light of reality much became clear.

There was no certainty that if they did leave New York her brothers and Phil and Fay would be allowed to live in peace. All that stood between them and their tormentors was Corelli's threat. When all was said and done, these people weren't afraid of Corelli anymore. They'd attacked him and killed his wife in the process. And Corelli's threat of tipping off the bank would simply enrage them even more. The consequences for all of them were unthinkable.

Her doubts were confirmed in the early hours of the next morning after Phil had gone to his nightshift at the warehouse. He had insisted on going because if he changed his routine, those who were watching would suspect that he was perhaps preparing to leave. There was no way of knowing how they'd react if they thought this was the case.

The racket at the apartment door had Nora out in the centre of the room before she was even half-awake. Soon the boys were standing petrified at their bedroom door. Fay rushed into the sitting room pulling on a dressing gown and wiping the sleep from her eyes. The knocking continued without pause.

'Go into your room and lock the door,' Fay whispered. 'You too, Nora.'

'We're staying with you,' Ritchie said firmly.

'Open up! Or we'll break the door in!'

There was no mistaking Danny Feeney's hate-filled twang.

'Just a minute,' Fay called and turned to Nora, 'Please, take the guys into the bedroom.'

'We can't leave you on your own,' Nora insisted.

With nervous fingers Fay brushed her hair back and went to the door. She stood to the side and opened it back. Danny Feeney came bursting in followed by a pint-sized man with heavy-lidded eyes and a big, bulging lower lip. There were no prizes for guessing that this was Danny's father. They were alike from the oily black slicked-back hair right down to the black shirts and white ties they both wore.

'Where's Phil?' Lefty Feeney asked in a pretence of politeness.

'He's out.'

'Check the rooms, Danny.'

'He's at the warehouse,' Fay insisted, 'You know that better than I do.'

'Just checking,' Lefty grinned.

He reached into his inside pocket and Nora gasped expecting him to produce a gun.

'Mind if I smoke?' he asked maliciously, taking out a cigarette packet.

'I got a message for your husband, sweetheart,' he went on, 'He's got the wrong kind of friends. Or maybe Corelli's *your* pal from your nightclub days. I bet you knew every hobo in town when you were on the skids.'

Fay's hands shook with rage. Feeney knew he was getting to her but he wasn't finished yet. He drew closer to her. They were almost the same height and his hot smoky breath ruffled her hair like a breeze from hell.

'You was an orphan, right?' he laughed, 'Tell me, what's it like not knowing what kind of sewer you was born in?'

Fay swung her fist in a neat uppercut to his weak chin and he shot back, bouncing his head against the wall. Danny made a lunge at Fay but before he could figure what had happened he was on the ground. Denis was kneeling across his legs and Ritchie sat astride his chest. In his hand, Ritchie held a penknife. He held the point to Danny's throat.

'What the...' Lefty yelled, holding his chin and trying to make sense of the scene around him, 'You let my kid go.'

'Not until you're out that door,' Ritchie shouted, 'And

don't think I won't hurt him. We've taken enough from you already. We ain't takin' no more.'

One look at Ritchie told Lefty he meant what he said.

'You're gonna pay for this, all of you,' Lefty warned, 'and none of your old pals is gonna stop us.'

He sidled away towards the door. Danny groaned beneath the point of Ritchie's knife.

'You can't leave me here,' he wailed.

'Aw, shut up,' Lefty bellowed. 'You people don't know what you started here. Nobody snatches half a million dollars from Harry and me and gets away with it. I got plans for my quarter million and you ain't gonna put a stop to 'em.'

Half a million dollars? Nora was sure she'd heard Phil tell Fay it was a million dollars.

'Half a million dollars,' Lefty repeated. 'I'd shoot that dumb kid of mine for half a million dollars. Now let him go.'

Denis and Ritchie jumped to their feet. Danny scrambled on his hands and knees after them but stopped dead as Ritchie waved the knife at him. He stood up and backed away, dusting himself off.

'You're dead meat,' he said, 'both of you. Say your prayers tonight and say plenty of 'em.'

'And you,' Lefty called to Nora, 'You ain't never gonna see your folks back home again. Write 'em a letter. Tell 'em goodbye.'

With the sound of the apartment door slammed shut ringing in their ears they stood around the sitting room in a state of shock. When Phil returned a half hour later they were waiting for him. His surprise soon turned to fury and his fury to a lost look of defeat.

'I guess,' he told Nora, 'you better talk to Corelli.'

The apartment settled down into an uneasy quietude as they drifted away to their rooms. Before long Nora, lying on her couch, heard Denis call softly from his bedroom door. She followed him in and closed the door quietly behind her.

'They're not going to let us leave New York, are they?' Denis asked.

'I thought you didn't know about all that.'

'We heard Phil and Fay talking about it,' Ritchie explained.

'But Feeney's not going to let us go, is he?' Denis asserted.

'I'll be meeting Corelli tomorrow, I'm sure he'll think of something,' she said, knowing she'd already asked too much of him.

What was he going to say when she told him, as she must, of Feeney's warnings? Would he have to decide that she wasn't worth the trouble?

'What's he really like? Corelli?' Denis wanted to know.

Nora was lost for an answer. What was he really like? Kind to a few, cruel to many?

'I don't know him well enough to say.'

'But he's got everything, hasn't he? Big car, big house, all that stuff?'

She gave him a warning glance. After all the trouble he'd got himself into, making a hero out of a gangster was the last thing he needed to do.

'Yes, he has plenty but I'll tell you something. Vincent Corelli is the saddest, unhappiest man I ever met,' she said firmly.

Denis lowered his eyes realising his blunder. From Ritchie's bed came the sound of chuckling to ease the tension. They looked at him wondering if he was laughing at them. He grinned up at them and explained.

'I was just thinking about the look on Danny's face when we got him on the ground.'

'Yeah,' Denis laughed, 'We really stood up to him, didn't we, Ritchie.'

'You can't leave me here,' Ritchie squealed, imitating Danny's tone of panic.

'I should've listened to you months ago, Ritchie. I should've stuck with you and he'd have left me alone.'

'Where did you learn to fight like that, Ritchie?' Nora wondered.

'You learn to take care of yourself, you don't need no gangs.'

'That's how it's gonna be with me from now on,' Denis declared.

It was good to see that they were no longer at each other's throats. Their future was uncertain still but at least they could face it together.

'We'll be rootin' for you tomorrow,' Ritchie told her.

'Nora?' Denis asked, 'Is...is Daddy really different now? Is he really a changed man?'

They'd been listening to what she'd said about their father as she argued with Phil. Nora recalled her description of him with regret. She was a user too, dragging up her father's past like that.

'Daddy wasn't a good father,' she began. 'He'd be the first to admit it himself and that's not an easy thing to do. Giving us up really broke his heart, believe me. I saw him a few weeks after you lads left and he looked like a ghost. You wouldn't have recognised him, his clothes were hanging off him. I saw him cry for you two and for me and Mam. But he knew he wouldn't be able to take care of us and Mam knew it too before she...before she died. It was her idea to ask Phil and Molly to take us and it's not maybe how we'd like it to be but it's for the best.'

'Why did she go and die on us, Nora?' Denis said, covering his eyes with his hands.

Nora moved towards him but he fell on to the bed beside Ritchie and hid his face in the blanket. It was pointless trying to think up some easy answer. There was none. She sat alongside her brothers on the bed. As if reading each other's minds their hands came together in the silence. All their thoughts were the same.

They were back in Inchicore and Mam was there as she always would be in their minds.

'You'll be alright before you're twice married,' she was saying, just as she always had when they were hurt or angry or sad.

And she was smiling. And they believed she would see them through this uncertain time too.

CHAPTER 18

Dawn's orange-red light was the colour of hope for Nora. As she lay waiting for the apartment to come alive she refused to consider anything but the most agreeable possibilities. Her hand would soon be back to normal and the boys would be on their way to a better life. It was as simple as that in the comfortable early hours, her palm tingling with a healing itch.

Only when Phil had left for work did she begin to stir. It was almost eight o'clock. In an hour she would be heading for the Brimstead Private Clinic. She dressed as quickly as her bandaged hand allowed and went to the kitchen. Fay was already there making the breakfast. Soon, Denis and Ritchie joined them.

Nora hadn't felt so good since her visit began and it was easy to convince herself that the tension and anxiety of the last few weeks had been worth it all for this one bright, happy-familied morning.

When they'd finished eating Fay called Nora into her bedroom. She went in fearfully hoping her aunt wasn't going to spoil this good feeling.

'Now, you can tell me to mind my own business if you like, Nora,' Fay began, 'But I been noticing those dresses you got ...I mean they're really pretty but...in this heat they're maybe too heavy. Know what I mean?'

She opened a wardrobe and fingered some dresses.

'I got some stuff here I never get to wear. And I'd like you to have this.'

She pulled out a light, pale green dress, so soft and silky you could roll it into a ball and never wrinkle it.

'I'm fine,' Nora said, her own dress feeling heavier than ever as she looked at the one her aunt was offering. 'I couldn't take it.'

'Hey, I bought it in a sale at Norton's on 14th Street,' Fay laughed, 'and when I got home I didn't like the colour. But on you it would be great.'

She left Nora to change into the dress which somehow made her feel older but she was glad of its coolness and loved the sleek touch of it. The boys whistled at her when she came out and Fay had to step between them and Nora, so vexed was she with embarrassment.

At ten minutes to nine they had all calmed down again and Nora and the boys went down to the front steps of the apartment house to wait for the taxi-cab. They watched the mailman make his deliveries along Wash-Basin Street. Even though it was warmer than ever out under the sun, people seemed to be going about their business with a lighter step than usual. It was as if they'd all woken with the same feeling Fay had described to Nora at breakfast. The radio weather forecast hadn't predicted a change but Fay had been quite sure that the stifling dog days were about to end. At least for a little while.

'Ritch. Denis. How you was?' the mailman called.

The boys introduced Nora and to her astonishment he held out a small package to her.

'Nora? I guess this must be for you, then,' he said and went on his way whistling out of tune.

Just then the cab arrived and there was no time to satisfy her brothers' curiosity. She slipped into the back seat and within moments she had left Wash-Basin Street.

The faulty letter 'a' on the typed name and address made it clear to her where the package had come from. She opened it and unwrapped the torn sheets of old newspaper. Inside was the pearl necklace the boys had given her. There, also, were the dollar bills Phil had given for the taxi fare home when she'd gone to the LaFonde building. She placed the necklace around her neck, avoiding the note with its proud letterhead. She expected nothing from it in any case, only a cruelly impersonal rejection. At last she read through it, quickly getting ready to crumple it up with her good hand. She read it again. And again.

Dear Miss Canavan,

Following your recent audition at this Foundation I have been requested to inform you of the Examiner's deliberations. The Examiner wishes to extend his compliments on the maturity and depth of your interpretations. However, he feels that you have yet a great distance to go to find that balance of ability and aspiration which is necessary to pursue a career in music.

In this respect, he feels that four years of study at this Foundation would be of great benefit to you. This period of study would include, in the third term, a six-month sojourn at the Paris Conservatoire and a similar interlude, during the final year, at another European city yet to be decided. At present, Vienna and Budapest are possible destinations.

Please contact this Foundation at your earliest convenience so that the necessary arrangements can be made.

The signature of the Countess LaFonde, though tiny, was nonetheless clear.

When Nora had recovered from her shock she felt a warm glow of pride. Her imagination ran riot — Paris, Vienna, Budapest! — then suddenly ground to a halt.

What if Corelli had simply forced the Count to accept her at the Foundation? Wasn't that how he'd got Stoneleigh to see her so quickly? But in the end, even these questions were of no real importance. For now that the offer had finally come, she knew that deep down she had no desire to stay in America. If music was all that mattered in her life then New York was the place for her right now...but how could you make anything but the most tragic of sounds if you were unhappy? The house in Stannix Lane with Molly and Peter was her home and she didn't want to leave it yet. It would of course be painful to leave the boys again, especially after what Denis had said — 'I don't know what I'll do when you go.' But she had confidence in Phil and Fay now.

Everything, she knew, depended on what happened in the next few hours. Would Corelli think of some way to solve the problem? And would the price then prove to be his absolute insistence that she stay in New York and study at the Foundation? Her only ray of hope was that when he'd brought her to the clinic the day before he had demanded nothing of her. He hadn't even mentioned the Foundation. Was that because he already knew the offer was in the post?

Disturbed by her confused thoughts, Nora caught a glimpse of the cab-driver's eyes in the rear-view mirror. She didn't like what she saw. No matter which way she moved his dark gaze seemed to follow her. Then, with a sudden turn of the steering wheel he brought the cab down a narrow lane and parked. Without a word he got out and went to a small door covered with graffiti.

Before the panic had time to set in, this door opened and Corelli and The Fist appeared. Corelli handed a set of number plates to the dark-eyed driver and got in beside Nora. The Fist took the wheel. Outside, the other man worked for a minute or two at the front and back ends of the cab.

'We gotta change the number plates,' Corelli told her. 'Can't be too careful. Hey, you're looking swell.'

The man knocked out a signal on the bonnet and they

drove out of the city towards Long Island. Their nervousness was infectious. The good early morning feeling was just a pale memory now. Nora's hand sent messages of alarm to her reeling brain.

'There's something I have to tell you, Mr Corelli.'

'Vincent,' he insisted.

'Sorry...Vincent. Last night, Lefty Feeney and his son came to the apartment. I think they're going to start a fight with your gang. And they're going to get us too.'

'You was right, Boss,' The Fist said.

'What does he mean?' Nora asked, her stomach sickeningly tight.

'One of our guys took a bullet in the leg last night,' Corelli mused calmly. 'I knew it had to be Feeney and Ruby.'

'What are you going to do?'

'I ain't figured it out yet. See, since I started trying to go straight and cut down my operation, I ain't got the manpower no more. The bottom line is, Ruby's got more guns. He's no dope, he knows that too. I can still take him, mind, but I'd lose a lot of good men. Maybe I don't find that easy to live with no more.'

'We can't let 'em walk all over us, Boss,' his assistant objected, 'The guys would die for you, you know that. And I'd be first in line.'

Corelli didn't, as Nora expected, turn on The Fist in rage. He was curiously calm and spoke as if his mind was elsewhere. In Europe, perhaps, with his daughter Maria. Or outside the Symphony Hall with a dying Oriana in his arms.

'Yeah, I know that.'

'I should never have come to you,' Nora cried, 'None of this would have happened if I hadn't...'

'Listen, you just get that kind of junk out of your head, kid,' he said. 'See, I broke the Golden Rule when I had you followed. I strayed into Ruby's territory. In this business that ain't allowed. But that was my decision and I ain't apologising to nobody for it.'

'But...'

'Forget it, Nora, you got a tough day ahead of you. In the meantime, maybe I'll find a way out of this mess. I don't wanna hear another word about it from you, right?'

The cab swept along the drive of the Brimstead Private Clinic disturbing the expensive haven of tranquillity. At the front porch, Corelli hesitated and looked around at the lush green grass and the splendid ranks of foliage.

'You go ahead, kid,' he smiled, 'I'll take a hike in the gardens here. Do some thinking. You're gonna be alright, ain't you?'

'I'll be fine,' she said and she wished Maria could see her father now, stripped of all his anger and his illusions of power. He handed The Fist a wad of money and patted him on the shoulder.

'Take care of things,' he told him and strolled off into the leafy depths.

As he dressed her wound Stoneleigh remained disturbingly quiet. Nora wondered if it was something to do with her hand or perhaps he was simply worried about whether he was going to be paid. From the moment she'd stepped into his surgery she'd felt awkward beneath his bespectacled frown. The bandaging completed he looked suddenly upward at her and asked sharply, 'Did Corelli buy that dress for you?'

She shook with indignation when she realised what he'd meant. What he was really asking was whether Corelli owned her soul now. She withdrew her hand from among the instruments and dressings on the table.

'My aunt gave this to me,' she protested and stood up to leave.

'I'm sorry,' he said, 'but I've seen so many young girls get mixed up with this type and they all turn out...well, let's just say they lose more than they ever gain.'

'I have my reasons for "mixing" with Mr Corelli.'

Immediately she was filled with an overpowering self-disgust. She had really descended among the 'users' now and had become the greatest user of all. She couldn't get out of the surgery fast enough. She fumbled with the door handle, angry with Stoneleigh, with herself, with Corelli. Brushing past The Fist in the waiting room she called over her shoulder to him.

'You better pay him quick. All he's interested in is his flippin' money.'

Stoneleigh had made her feel small but her own words only made the feeling worse. She'd read a story once about a man selling his soul to the devil and she didn't like to think what happened at the end. It seemed to her that every person she passed in the corridor was staring at her as if to ask: 'Look at her hand, she was supposed to lose that hand, how did she save it, what desperate promises did she make and to whom and will she keep them?'

When The Fist caught up with her at the clinic entrance he was too irate to notice her demented state.

'Some nerve that guy has,' he railed, 'Prices like that, the guy should be in jail.'

Nora wasn't listening. She wanted to confront Corelli.

'He's a bigger crook than I ever was,' he yelled to the bemused patients and nurses within earshot.

Outside under the blazing sun he scanned the gardens but there was no sign of Corelli. He reached into his pocket and pulled out a pistol.

'For God's sake, put the gun away,' Nora raged, 'there's sick people out here.'

He slipped it back into his jacket but held a grip on it.

Hurrying along the pebbled walk he almost collided with

an old woman in a wheelchair who shook her fist weakly at him. As soon as he was out of sight, Corelli appeared at the opposite end of the building. So submerged in his thoughts was he that, at first, he didn't see her.

'Mr Corelli,' she called, wondering how she could ever have let herself call him by his first name.

She watched him darkly as he approached, his baggy suit flapping in the slight breeze, the twitch in his eye slowly working itself into a frenzy.

'What is it, kid?' he asked, 'Bad news?'

'Do you think you own me? Well, do you?'

Corelli reeled back as if he'd taken a blow. His left eye flickered but the right was fixed on her in disbelief. A voice screamed in her head telling her she was putting everything at risk because of her hurt pride. But she had to have an answer.

'Well, do you?'

He lowered his head and the oversized hat threw his face into shadow. He kicked gently at a pebble that stood out from all the rest, the sun glinting along its silvery vein.

'I got the cash to buy any damn thing I want,' he said, studying the little stony light at his toe cap, 'but I found out, the hard way, that there's nothing, nothing I can really own. Pretty soon these income tax guys will take my house, every nickel I ever put together, everything I ever bought. And I thought I owned Oriana and Maria as well, owned them like they were mine and I was theirs. But that's gone too.'

There was a blankness in his gaze now, the twitching of his eye a mere flutter.

'And you, kid. I never wanted to own you but I guess I can't blame you for thinking that way.'

Nora floundered almost drunkenly towards a bench alongside the clinic steps. Covering her face she grimaced at the thought of her insensitivity. Corelli came and sat beside her.

'Hey, I'm dumb but I'm no fool,' he said. 'I know you got problems accepting help from a guy like me.'

'It's not like that,' she lied.

'Sure it is,' he said, 'Let's be straight. Even if you was offered a place at that Foundation you wouldn't really want to take it, would you?'

'You didn't make them take me, did you?' she asked despairingly.

'I wouldn't do that.'

'I'm still thinking about it but I can't make a decision until they write, can I?'

She could scarcely believe what she was saying, so astounded was she that she was still holding back, still unwilling to be totally honest with him.

'I guess not but try to see it this way. Here's a pretty mean guy doing the right thing for once in his life. Maybe when I meet the "Big Guy in the Sky",' he laughed, 'He'll say, "You wasn't all bad, Corelli." You'll think about me sometimes, kid, won't you? When they put me six feet under?'

The sun wasn't warm anymore.

'You shouldn't be talking like that,' Nora objected. 'If anything happens to you now, I'll know it's my fault.'

'Hey, you got it all wrong,' he said. 'You think Ruby and Feeney are the only enemies I got? This city is full of guys who want to take a shot at me. So far I been lucky, if you can call losing your family any kind of luck. But one day, one of these guys will get lucky. It's gonna happen, nothing surer. And if they don't get me, the income tax guys will have me. And that means a long stretch in jail. I ain't sure if I wouldn't prefer to take a bullet.'

'Why can't you just get out and start a new life somewhere else?'

'Too late, kid, I'm in too deep. There ain't no place in the whole United States I'd be safe.'

'You could leave America altogether.'

'Here, I'm somebody. Kind of important, if you like. Anywhere else, I'd be a nobody. That I couldn't take.'

'What's wrong with being a nobody?'

He smiled a thin grim smile.

'Do you want to be a nobody?' he asked, 'OK, you play the music 'cause you like to but there's more, ain't there? Be honest now, d'ye really wanna hide away in some little room and play that piano all for yourself? Or do you wanna get out there in front of lots of folks and let them see how good you are? You want to be a somebody too, right?'

It seemed as if he'd looked into her very soul. It was true that all performers were, in a sense, show-offs but it wasn't something you wanted to admit to yourself. Even now, she thought, she was performing. One last act, one last question, one last favour. For the boys' sake, because she loved them more than she hated herself.

'Have you thought over what you're going to do about Ruby?' she asked.

From somewhere nearby came the ground-shaking thumps of The Fist's footsteps. His big, battered face had taken another bruising. His coat sleeve dangled by a few threads from the shoulder.

'I just ran into some trouble!' he shouted as he ran, 'Get in the car!'

They raced across the driveway and piled in. Like a shot out of a gun, the car sped away with pebbles flying in all directions from the spinning tyres.

'One of Ruby's?' Corelli asked peering through the back window.

'Two of 'em,' The Fist chortled. 'They're gonna be asleep for a while.'

'Are they dead?' Nora cried.

'No,' the big man grinned, 'but when they wake up they're

gonna wish they were.'

'A rat, that's what Ruby is, nothing more,' Corelli hissed. 'How can I send you to him now?'

'What do you mean?'

'Some crazy idea I got into my head, but I can't trust that guy. He'd shoot his own grandmother.'

The car rocked from side to side as The Fist swerved it in and out of the traffic.

'You were going to send me to see Ruby?' Nora gasped, dizzy from the speed of the swaying car.

'It was stupid. If he wants a fight, that's what he's gonna get.'

'Looks like we're clear, Boss,' The Fist said as he slowed down to the pace of the other cars on the road.

'I guess I owe you one,' Corelli said.

'You don't owe me nothing, Boss. You took me outa the gutter and...'

'Ah forget it.'

Corelli stretched his neck back and closed his eyes. He didn't look like he was thinking. He looked like he didn't want to think anymore.

'What was your plan?' Nora asked.

'I guess I was gonna use you to get myself out of a hole. I been doing that all my life with people.'

'Just tell me,' she pressed, seizing the chance to redeem herself.

'See, I thought if I could arrange for you to meet Ruby, you could...you could explain that I crossed into his territory just so's I could help you, not because I wanted to take over his operation. Then...hey, this is crazy.'

'Then what?'

'I was gonna have you make him an offer. I forget what he did to Oriana and he forgets the million dollars I screwed up on him. It's a bit of a long shot but I know he really did feel bad about what happened to my wife. It ain't easy for me to admit that but I thought if I can bend a little, so can he. I thought maybe he could let your folks go out Midwest too. Seems to me like a small price to pay for the life of a good woman. A million dollars, that's just pocket money to a guy like that.'

Again the words 'one million dollars' clanged in her head like an out-of-tune note. Why had Phil and now Corelli mentioned *one* million dollars when Feeney had said repeatedly, *half* a million?

'I'll go. It's the least I can do for you.'

Corelli sat up straight and considered the skyline of the fast-approaching city.

'I can't let you, I gotta be honest, I was just trying to avoid a fight....'

'I'm not doing it for you, I'm doing it for my brothers.'

She hadn't meant it like it sounded but he stared at her so coldly that she knew it had hurt him deeply.

'I mean I want to repay you too but my brothers come first.'

Within minutes, The Fist was in a cafe, making the phone call to Ruby. Nora and Corelli waited in the car. Corelli was very quiet. It seemed to Nora that he'd realised he hadn't found a replacement for Maria in her. His eyes were the eyes of a man who has given up all interest in life.

Soon, his assistant was standing by the car and Corelli opened down the window.

'Just me and the kid, he says. He'll have Feeney with him.'

'That OK with you?' Corelli asked.

'Sure, I can handle the both of 'em if we get a problem,' The Fist muttered, crunching his knuckles.

'Where's it to be?'

'Al Hagen's Bar.'

Corelli turned to Nora. 'You can back out now, I ain't gonna push you.'

'I'm ready,' Nora said. 'But before we go to the bar, can you take me to the First Mutual Bank? I have to see my uncle.'

He looked at her uncertainly.

'I promise I won't tell him what's going on.'

'Sure. You got it.'

One million dollars, *half* a million dollars. The off-key echo refused to go away. As if she had stumbled over something in the dark, the hair on the nape of her neck bristled.

There was, after all, something Phil could do. The most important thing was whether her idea would work but she was glad to be able to give her uncle the opportunity to salvage some of his battered pride.

At the bank Phil grudgingly handed over the single sheet he'd sneaked from the files, and Nora wondered if something so flimsy could really have the spectacular effect she hoped for. As she stepped back on to the street she saw Corelli get out of the car. He reached out his hand and she took it. He didn't speak. The Fist sat in behind the wheel. All around them the city throbbed like some hot beast bearing down on its victim.

CHAPTER 19

The bar was a narrow, dingy place. It reeked of the stale remains of what some regard as 'good times'. Behind the long bar counter stood a sullen, sleepy-eyed man with a vast unkempt crop of moustache. On top of his balding head was a deep ugly groove, the relic of some long-ago brawl.

'I don't want no trouble,' he said gruffly.

'Beat it, Al,' The Fist told him, 'Go back to bed.'

The bar owner thought about squaring up to The Fist but quickly backed down. He lumbered away through a small door behind the counter. Nora and The Fist watched impatiently the door they'd come in by.

'Do you think Ruby will listen to me?' she asked.

The big man shrugged. After all the intrigue and danger of the last week, it all came down now to this one meeting. And the slip of paper Phil had given her at the bank just ten minutes ago. The long wait before a music exam was never anything like this. It was like Judgement Day but instead of God, Satan himself was about to pass sentence.

The door handle turned. The Fist stood up suddenly. He dipped his hand into his coat pocket and left it there.

'Get behind me, kid,' he whispered and she obeyed without question.

The door swung open but all they could see was the alleyway behind. Seconds ticked by.

'I'm coming in.'

Lefty Feeney stepped into the doorway. Like The Fist, he had one hand deep in his coat pocket.

'Hey, we agreed there'd be no shooters,' Feeney croaked.

'Guns on the counter,' The Fist commanded.

'Sure, no problem.'

'When your friend is inside,' added The Fist.

Now the doorway darkened again and an impeccably-dressed man stood with a coat thrown over his shoulders. His gloved hands were held out before him. His deeply-tanned face was wrinkled before its time from too much sun. He was darkly handsome in an untrustworthy kind of way.

'For now,' he said, 'we're all friends, am I right?'

He strode over to the bar counter.

'No deal,' The Fist replied. 'I ain't droppin' my piece 'til I see yours.'

The line of Ruby's jaw hardened.

'Sure. Feeney? You got him covered?' he snarled.

'I got him covered.'

Ruby slipped a small pearl-handled gun from his loosely-hanging coat and left it on the bar counter. He strolled across and sat at a table filthy with cigarette ash and beer glasses, stained with the frothy dregs of last night's drinking.

'Don't this guy ever clean up?' Ruby complained and swept his hand across the table, sending the glasses and ashtray smashing to the floor. 'Danny?'

'Yeah?' came the familiar voice from outside.

'Get in here.'

Danny wasn't his usual brash self. As he hurried towards Ruby, his eyes met Nora's and he looked quickly away. He didn't like being treated like a small boy in her presence.

'You said there was gonna be two of you,' The Fist objected.

'Aw, he's just a kid,' Ruby grinned, 'We just took him along for the ride.'

'You got a shooter, kid?' The Fist asked him threateningly.

Danny was a bundle of nerves. His mouth moved but no sound came.

'Let the guy check you out, Danny,' Ruby said and Danny moved towards The Fist with his arms raised.

'Alright, forget it,' The Fist blustered. 'OK Feeney, we move together and we drop the pieces, you got it?'

When all the guns were on the bar counter, The Fist called out Al's name. The bar owner came scuttling in, the scar on his skull quivering feverishly.

'Take care of these, Al.'

He beat a hasty retreat, his clammy hands wrapped around the guns. The small group sat around the ash-strewn table. Nora's stomach twisted into an uncomfortable knot. Ruby brushed the grey hair at his temples with a well-manicured finger. He liked himself. A lot.

'OK, so convince me. Tell me why I shouldn't believe Vincent isn't trying to cut in on my territory.'

The Fist began, 'The kid has something to say to you and—'

'Excuse me,' Ruby interjected in a treacly voice, 'I don't believe we've been introduced.'

'Uh...sure...' The Fist stuttered, 'Nora Canavan. Harry Ruby.'

Ruby made quite a display of getting to his feet and offering his hand. Nora took it. There was nothing to gain and everything to lose by showing her dislike of him.

'A pleasure to make your acquaintance,' he said, and sat down again, very impressed with himself.

'I must apologise for the circumstances of our meeting. And the surroundings.'

Nora struggled to begin. All eyes were on her now and her throat was dry in the evil atmosphere.

'Tell you what,' Ruby said to the others, 'Why don't you

guys get on over there and have yourselves a drink on me.'

'That OK with you, kid?' The Fist asked.

'Grand,' she muttered. Though she would certainly have preferred to have him alongside her, she was glad to escape the close leering presence of Lefty and Danny. Ruby's foot tapped impatiently and without rhythm on the sodden floor.

'I wanted to explain...' she began.

'Did Corelli put you up to this?'

'No,' she lied, 'It was my idea.'

'Why would you want to help him?'

'I'm not doing this for him. I'm doing it for my brothers.'

He sat back heaving a sigh of exasperation.

'You're not making sense, kid.'

'If you give me a chance to talk,' she said, getting flustered, 'you might understand.'

'I can tell you're no pushover,' he sneered.

'I came over her to America a few weeks ago,' she said, 'and on the ship one night I was playing the piano, and...'

'You're a musician,' he declared.

'Yes, I suppose I am,' she affirmed, 'and Mr Corelli heard me and offered to send me to the LaFonde Musical Foundation.'

She went on to explain that Corelli had had her followed in Ruby's 'territory' only because he wanted to see if she'd take up his offer. She told him about the boys and why they were living with Phil and the desperate situation they now found themselves in. As for Corelli's interference in the bank robbery plan, that was, she explained, her fault because she'd asked him to help her uncle. All Phil wanted was to leave New York with his family to start a new life.

'All very reasonable,' Ruby acknowledged and Nora felt elated. 'Very reasonable indeed,' he continued, 'but I got problems with it. For one, Feeney's one of my best men, he does good work for me. Two — the way I see it your uncle owes us some money. And thirdly, I need to know why I should say goodbye to half a million dollars, just like that.'

He clicked his fingers and shrugged nonchalantly.

'I have to say I am not convinced but I gotta hand it to you, you're a brave kid for trying.'

Hunched forward, her voice lowered, Nora told him that Phil had paid the loan back many times over. He showed no sign of emotion.

'And that money you were going to steal from the bank. Feeney told you it was half a million dollars, didn't he?'

'You're losing me again,' he said but his suspicion was aroused.

'It wasn't half a million dollars,' she said, 'It was a million dollars.'

Ruby guffawed and slapped his knee. 'I gotta hand it to Vincent,' he laughed, 'He's trying to set me against my own guys.'

The others turned their heads towards them. Lefty and Danny chuckled though they had no idea what the joke was. The Fist glared malevolently at Ruby. Nora reached into her pocket and produced the piece of paper Phil had given her. Lefty and Danny went quiet. Ruby himself paled visibly as he grabbed the sheet from her hand. He was forgetting his manners. He read slowly, his brow furrowing ever deeper as he took in its contents.

Under the headings, 'First Mutual Bank' and 'Notice of Deposit' was the date and time of the deposit, the name of the company, Sitron Inc. and the unmistakable figure of *one million dollars*. It was clear he was having difficulty coming to terms with what he read.

'Lefty's been double-crossing me,' he muttered, 'I gotta check this out. You're coming with me.'

They stood up to go. The Fist swung around into a fighting position.

'The kid stays with me,' he said firmly.

'It's alright,' she told him, 'I trust Mr Ruby.'

'She has nothing to fear from me,' he said and fixing his glare on Lefty and Danny added, 'I don't push ladies around. I treat them with respect.'

Danny looked down at his two-toned shoes. Lefty stared at the whiskey bottles behind the bar like he wanted to break every one of them. Through the rubbish-filled alleyway Nora followed Ruby until they reached another door as grimy as the one leading into Al Hagen's Bar.

She caught a glimpse of the sky and for the first time since she'd come to this city, it was not clear blue. A muddy brown cloud seeped into view. Ruby's shadow disappeared and Nora's too, swallowed up in the grey grime beneath their feet.

Ruby pushed the door in and they entered another seedy drinking den. It was empty but Ruby seemed to know his way around it. He made straight for the phone. In a dusty alcove which had never seen the sun and would have crumbled apart if it ever had, he paused before picking up the mouthpiece. He cleaned it with a silk handkerchief and asked to be put through to the offices of Sitron Inc.

'Good day, Madam. May I speak to your accounts manager? This is the First Mutual Bank. Thank you.'

As he waited to speak to the accounts manager he eyed Nora in such a menacing way that her blood ran cold.

'You better hope this isn't one of Corelli's tricks,' he threatened, and then brightening up returned to his call. 'Ah, yes, Mr...? Orrtell, right. See, I'm new here. Listen, we're just running a check on your lodgement today. Thing is I've got this assistant and she's, let's just say, a little slow. We'd like to know if you've got your statement yet for the lodgement. We aim to give the best service we can to our top depositors and, let's face it, half a million dollars makes your company an important customer. Oh, right. A million dollars. Like I said, I'm new here, I got some catching up to do. But you got the statement, great. Sorry for bothering you. Yeah, sure, I'll be talking to you again.'

His face drawn, he slammed down the phone. Suddenly, Nora had a new worry to contend with. As much as she despised Lefty and Danny, she didn't want to see them murdered. Right now, murder was what was in Ruby's eyes.

'You're not going to kill them because of what I told you, are you?'

'I haven't decided yet.'

'Are you going to call off the war with Corelli?' she asked desperately.

He considered the matter for what seemed an unbearably long time in the hot clammy alcove. Then he spoke in measured tones.

'Even if Feeney did try to sucker me,' he said, 'We're still talking about a lotta dollars I should have in my pocket right now.'

It was time to play the final card in this cruel game. She braced herself as if to fire her last arrow into his heart. The trouble was she couldn't be sure if he had any heart at all.

'Did you love Oriana Corelli?'

Ruby held his breath. The deep tan on his bloodless face turned a sickly yellow-brown.

'I never meant to kill her, Vincent knows that.'

'But you did love her once, didn't you?'

'She walked out on me.'

'Is money more important than Oriana? A half million dollars *or* a million?'

'What d'ye mean?'

'Mr Corelli says he'll take your word it was a mistake if you call your men off,' she explained. 'He wants to know if you think Oriana was worth giving up a million dollars for.'

Ruby sat back, dumbstruck.

'He knows you didn't mean to kill her.'

'He does?' Ruby said, his frown changing into something like a smile. 'Vincent is a smart guy. If anybody was going to convince me, it had to be someone like you.'

Nora waited for his decision. Though she was looking straight at him all she could see was her brothers' young faces.

'And, hey, I'm convinced. Him and me, we're never gonna be friends but you can tell him this. If he sticks to his own side of town, he won't have no trouble from me. And tell him ...Oriana...'

He turned his face slowly away from her and just as slowly wheeled it back around again. He almost spoke but couldn't put the right words together.

'I know what to tell him,' Nora said.

'Right,' he seethed, brightening up, 'about your kid brothers and this uncle of yours, they're free to go whenever they want to.'

'What about Lefty and Danny?' she asked.

'I guess Mr Feeney will be leaving New York too,' he said, 'except he'll be leaving the United States. He comes inside five thousand miles of me, he's dead.'

They left the vile-smelling pit and walked the short distance to Al Hagen's Bar. Claps of thunder growled in the strange twilight of a mid-afternoon. At the door he swung around so quickly to her that she thought he'd had a change of heart.

'I've been meaning to ask — what happened to your hand?'

'It was an accident...at the apartment.'

'Not Feeney or that punk kid of his?'

'No.'

'You sure?' he asked sharply, 'These guys don't deserve protecting.'

'I'm sure, really.'

'OK,' he said but his eyes were so darkly vengeful she knew Lefty and Danny were not yet safe from his pent-up fury.

Droplets of filthy moisture spat from the dead sky until one last rasp of thunder echoed in the alleyway and a hellish rain pelted down mercilessly on them. Ruby pushed open the door hurriedly.

'Lefty!' he yelled, 'Get over here. You got some explaining to do.'

CHAPTER 20

The whiskey glass in Lefty Feeney's hand slipped from his grasp and dropped to the floor. The Fist never flinched but Nora could see the muscles of his arms flexed in readiness. Danny looked first at his terror-stricken father and then at Nora. His eyes were filled with a fierce hatred.

'You been listening to her lies, Harry,' Lefty complained as he approached with mincing steps. 'I don't know what she's been sayin' but it ain't true.'

His teeth tightly clamped together, Ruby ground words out of his mouth like meat from a mincer.

'You don't get to call me Harry no more,' he said. 'Can you count, Lefty?'

'Sure, I can count.'

'So tell me, how do you make half a million outa a million?'

'I always done my best for you, Ha...Mr Ruby. I ain't never let you down. Why would I want to do it now?'

'I been asking myself the same question,' Ruby told him, 'and I don't like the answers I'm gettin'.'

Lefty was within three feet of Ruby now and his face suddenly brightened as he noticed his boss had begun to smile. But it was the smile of a spider and Lefty was the fly.

'You believe me, don't you?' Lefty pleaded, 'Whatever she's been sayin', it's all a bunch of...'

Ruby's gloved fist met Lefty's mouth with a splintering

crack. Hitting the floor, Lefty curled himself into a ball expecting the worst. And it came. Ruby's foot smashed into his stomach and he dragged himself further across the floor. The next kick found the small of his back.

Nora looked over at The Fist. He shook his head as if to tell her what she already knew. If he tried to stop Ruby it could mean war between the rival gangs. Another sickening thud filled the bar. A shiver ran down Nora's spine. Then, something very cold touched her temple.

'Ruby!' Danny Feeney shouted, his gun held shakily to Nora's head, 'Back off or I shoot.'

The Fist rose slowly from his bar stool as Ruby turned to face Danny. 'Put it down, kid,' he said calmly.

'You think I won't shoot,' Danny exclaimed, yanking Nora's arm back as he'd done at the old bathhouse. 'Pop, are you alright? Get behind me, come on.'

Lefty raised himself to his knees and spat out on to the floor a horrific mixture of congealed blood and broken teeth. He rose waveringly but couldn't stand up straight. Danny twisted Nora's arm so painfully that she cried out. The Fist made to run at him but Danny lifted the gun and fired off a round into the ceiling. Ruby cowered away, ducking for cover behind an overturned table. The Fist stood in the centre of the bar, refusing to back down.

'See what he did,' Danny cried, 'You're gonna be OK Pop. Just get to the door.'

'Danny,' Lefty groaned, 'Put the gun down. We're in deep enough as it is.'

'I ain't afraid of that Flash Harry,' Danny yelled, 'Now, come on, we're outa here.'

'Forget it, Danny,' Lefty said, 'I can't walk, how am I gonna run?'

The gun sank deeper into Nora's cheek. The metallic coldness was gone and the barrel burned her skin. Danny let go of her arm and fumbled around behind him for the door handle.

'Hand over the gun, kid,' The Fist repeated, 'I promise we won't touch you. Right, Ruby?'

'Yeah, sure,' Ruby said, looking far from cool now as he skulked behind the table. 'The kid got excited is all.'

Only a fool would have believed him. Danny found the door handle and pushed it back. He moved outside with his arm now wrapped roughly around Nora's neck. It was like stepping under a waterfall, the rain poured so heavily. As they retreated, the back door of Al Hagen's Bar disappeared as if behind some watery screen.

'Anyone follows me,' Danny roared above the noise of the downpour, 'and she's had it!'

Only yards from the door Nora, in her light silky dress, was already soaked to the skin. The voices from inside the bar came like murmurs from some unearthly world. There was no question of kicking out or swinging her elbows back at Danny. The gun, drilled menacingly into her cheek, saw to that.

'Where are you taking me?' she shouted above the ear-splitting din.

'Shut your face!' Danny yelled and Nora knew he had no idea what to do next.

'If you let me go, you'll get away quicker.'

'Aw, belt up, I don't need no guff from you.'

He was growing more uncertain with every backward step. This made him even more dangerous, more likely to make another mistake. Like pulling that trigger his finger pressed so excitedly on.

Nora knew the alleyway couldn't last forever. Soon they would have to emerge on to the street. Surely there, someone would come to her rescue? Then again, was anyone likely to be out walking beneath these torrents of rain? It was almost impossible for Nora to keep her eyelids open, the rain battered them so savagely. When Danny's grip on her neck loosened she was too blinded to see why.

In an instant, the gun wasn't pressing against her skin and Danny's jumpy breath wasn't echoing in her ear. She turned full circle but couldn't see him in the splashing haze. She thought he must have made a run for it. Then two figures came into view in a doorway nearby. She ran towards them thinking it must be The Fist and Ruby.

'You alright, Nora?' her uncle Phil called as he held Danny Feeney up against the doorway.

'Let me go,' Danny pleaded.

'You were holding a gun to Nora's head, you little punk,' Phil yelled, lifting him by his shirt front.

'I wasn't gonna hurt her, honest. I just had to get outa there!'

Danny peered over Phil's shoulder at Nora.

'You saw what he did to my old man,' he cried, 'You know what he's like. I got to get away.'

Nora knew she could have her revenge on Danny now for all he'd done to her and Denis. All she had to do was have Phil hand him over to Ruby. Ruby would gladly do the rest. But she couldn't let herself do it. Not after seeing Lefty being beaten up.

'Let him off, Phil,' Nora said.

'But the guy...'

'I've seen what Ruby can do. He's a monster,' she told him.

From the direction of Al Hagen's Bar came the broken-down call of Danny's father. The words were barely distinguishable.

'Danny? You still out there? Danny?'

A blood-smeared face peered anxiously around the corner of the grimy doorway.

'Danny? Mr Ruby says we can talk this out.'

Phil's grip on the boy was loosening as he stared at Lefty's ruined face.

'It ain't half so bad as it seems, Danny. Hey, it don't even hurt no more. Come on, kid, come inside, let's talk.'

'My old man,' Danny was whispering to himself as he listened to his father's craven plea.

He looked at Nora. There was a terrible sadness in his eyes. It was as if he'd seen his greatest hero reduced to a whimpering, bleeding shadow. Then a deeper voice from behind them filled the painful silence.

'Do like he says, son,' The Fist advised, his huge bulk blocking off any chance of escape for Danny.

Dragging his arm away from Phil, Danny stood for a quiet moment adjusting his tie and sweeping back the lock of hair which had fallen over his forehead. Suddenly he shot a glance beyond The Fist into the busy street, already pulsating with traffic after the downpour.

'It's the cops!' he cried and as The Fist spun around, Danny made a break for it.

He was by the big man in an instant, Lefty's roar ringing in his ears.

'No, Danny! Don't run! There ain't no place to run to!'

But Danny was already across the pavement and, by now, was lunging out onto the street. He almost made it to the other side. When the car hit him he was within two feet of the far sidewalk.

The Fist was the first to reach the twisted bundle that was once Danny Feeney. Phil held Nora back and drew her close as the tension and grief of these last hours spilled out from her. But above her loud cries she could hear Lefty's baleful screams.

She looked over Phil's shoulder and saw Lefty clutch his son's broken body to himself.

'Danny. Wake up. Talk to me, Danny.'

The Fist put his hand on the grieving man's arm and shook his head.

'Get your filthy mitts offa me,' Lefty cried, 'You killed him, you and that stinking wop, Corelli. We was gonna start up our own operation, me and the kid, with that dough from the bank. He coulda been the tops, the number one, the...'

Fixing his hat over his sleek head, Harry Ruby strolled into view.

'What's with the kid?' he asked offhandedly of Phil.

'The boy is dead,' Phil said and gritted his teeth as their stares locked together dangerously.

Nora held on tightly to her uncle as if this might staunch the flow of hate and disgust in him. The wrong word spoken now would bring the shaky facade of freedom tumbling down.

'Pity,' Ruby mumbled pitilessly.

Phil inhaled sharply but Lefty's animal cry from among the gathering crowd of bystanders intervened before there was time to speak.

'They killed him, Harry...Mr Ruby. They killed the kid. They're gonna pay.'

From the edge of the sidewalk Ruby called loud enough for everyone to hear.

'You leave these people out of it, Lefty,' he warned, nodding towards Phil and Nora. 'We got a deal with Corelli. I don't want no more trouble, see?'

Cradling his son in his arms, Lefty looked around pleading for sympathy from the curious crowd, more interested now in the loud conversation than in the dead boy.

'I ain't talkin' about them people,' he said quietly.

'Well, you just remember that,' Ruby said, 'and hey, Lefty.'

'Yeah?'

'Send the funeral bill round to me. I'll go halves on it with you.'

'Thanks, Boss,' Lefty moaned and spat out a shard of

cracked tooth into the gutter.

Ruby turned his attention to Phil. His cruel leer was clearly designed to provoke trouble.

'Give the hicks out Midwest my regards,' he said and sauntered away.

Phil took a step away from Nora but she pulled him back. When he looked at her it was clear he was glad she'd done it. Ruby turned the corner and was gone from their lives.

In the distance a police siren sounded. The Fist rose from Lefty's side and shuffled across the street between the stationary cars.

'Best clear outa here fast,' he told Nora, 'We'll send a cab for you tomorrow, OK?'

'What for?' Phil objected.

'She's gotta go to the clinic again.'

'I'll take my niece wherever she needs to go.'

Nora stood between the two men. She couldn't help feeling how petty this little argument was compared to the infinitely sad scene on the street. That might well have been Denis' destiny, she told herself. No one deserved to die like that, not even Danny Feeney who, in the end, was merely a boy. A boy who never had a chance to live any other life than one of crime and violence.

There was something odd about the pathetic sight of Lefty and Danny. Lefty, bruised and bloodied was alive and his son lay dead with no visible mark on his young face. It was almost as if death was easier than life sometimes.

'It doesn't matter how I get to the clinic.'

Phil and The Fist looked at each other shamefacedly.

'Sure,' The Fist said, 'but you'll be in touch with the Boss, won't you? 'Bout the music business?'

'Of course,' she said, her voice constricted, the noose of her responsibilities seeming to tighten around her throat.

'I'll give you the phone number.' He smiled and wrote it

on an old cinema ticket, the pencil stub tiny in his thick, muscular fingers. 'You won't forget now? Jamica 3500, OK?'

A faint breeze coursed through from the alleyway behind and Nora shivered in her wet dress. Phil slipped off his brown leather jacket and placed it over her shoulders. A police car turned the corner onto the street and without a further word, The Fist parted company with them. They walked in the opposite direction and eventually found a yellow cab to take them back to Wash-Basin Street.

In the line of traffic, slowed to a crawl by Danny's accident, the cab made little progress. Nora's trembling continued in spite of the warmth of Phil's jacket. Her mind veered wildly between the joy of her brothers' release from their torment and sadness at Danny's death, at all death.

She knew that Phil must be wondering what all this talk of the 'music business' was about. Her explanation, as confused as it was, at least rescued her from her brooding.

'Seems to me,' Phil said, when she'd finished the story of the morning's events, 'you don't need to worry about the Foundation now. He did you a favour, you did him a favour. So you're quits.'

'I suppose so.'

The rain had stopped altogether now and already the sun was drying out the streets. A shimmering haze rose from every car bonnet and roof. The air was filled with a fresh vitality though it was still warm. Nora's trembling subsided.

'These guys really had me on the ropes,' Phil told her, 'and I could see no way out but their way. But when you came to the bank this morning you gave me the chance to start picking myself up. Maybe all I did was find a piece of paper and take a gun from some poor misguided kid but it was something. At least I can feel I've done my bit to get us out of this hole.'

The taxi-cab began to move more quickly now. It seemed like the world had already forgotten Danny Feeney. But Phil hadn't.

'You know, I been thinking,' he said. 'That kid, Danny, for all the trouble he caused us I never felt he was really bad. He was just a young kid gone wild. Even Lefty and that guy, The Fist. But Ruby, he's different, I mean you just feel it when he's around, don't you? A real icy cold. That was the first time I ever felt like I was in the presence of evil.'

'Mr Corelli isn't like that either,' Nora insisted quietly, 'That's why I find it so hard to tell him I'm not going to the Foundation.'

'Do it soon, Nora. If you put it off it'll get even harder.'

'Maybe tomorrow.'

Their arrival back at the apartment was filled with great elation. Phil told Fay and the boys they were on their way to Dennsville and they stayed up very late talking excitedly about the future.

'I guess we ain't gonna see no more dog days in New York,' Fay declared.

'From every mountainside let freedom ring,' Phil added grandly.

The boys moaned cheerfully as he went on to recite the rest of the poem, ignoring their best efforts to quieten him. When he'd finished and they'd stopped jeering he told them the poem was called 'America'.

'No amount of Harry Rubys will take away my faith in this country. I got a second chance here from the slums of Dublin. Now, thanks to Nora, I get yet another one.'

Ritchie and Denis were silenced by his heartfelt outburst. His words carried the same truth for them.

'Fay,' Phil beamed, 'Break open some soda pop. Let's drink a toast. To the Land of the Second Chance.'

A cheer went up again as their glasses were filled with the fizzy water Nora had never got used to. It seemed as if there was plenty of time to tell Corelli of her decision. The urgency of it all was lost in the celebrations.

Maybe the day *after* tomorrow, she told herself. Or even later, when her treatment was finished at the end of the week. There was all the time in the world. And he would understand. He had already said as much. And the delay would prepare him.

All the time in the world.

CHAPTER 21

At last Nora began to enjoy a real holiday. Each day, Fay and the boys took her out to see the sights of New York while Phil worked out his week's notice of leaving the bank. The same streets she'd wandered in the lonely confusion of these last weeks seemed less frenetic now that the danger had passed. It was as if she was seeing the city for the first time and her former impressions of it the imagined labyrinth of nightmare.

What before had seemed gigantically intimidating was now grandly spectacular. Central Park, a vast oasis of green tranquillity at the heart of the concrete chaos. The nearby Museum of Natural History with its fascinating array of birds, fish, reptiles and insects traced the evolution of life from its distant beginnings in the mud and slime of ancient seas. On a lighter note they visited an impressive art gallery where Ritchie and Denis had great fun smirking at the half-dressed ladies of Gauguin.

Most breathtaking of all was the Woolworth Building, the tallest in the world at 729 feet. Its terracotta Gothic facade rose from the street to an elegant, if barely visible spire. They went to the top in a terrifying moving contraption called an elevator and looked out at the view over the city. Nora marvelled at the courage of those who'd climbed to such a height to meld stone and metal together. Even looking out by a window she had to grip the sill such was her dizzy terror at being so far above the street.

There were some night-time trips too, the best of which was when they went to see the latest Mary Pickford film, *Dorothy Vernon of Hadden Hall*. It would be at least two years before this one would reach Tipperary. The thought of seeing it so soon after its release thrilled Nora. Instead of the lone piano of the Stella Cinema at home a five-piece orchestra accompanied the action on that special night.

The film too held a surprise for Nora. Mary Pickford was by far her favourite star. Invariably she played the part of a young almost tomboyish girl who through sheer guts and quick thinking overcame all the odds stacked against her. This time, however, though still a survivor her role was that of a young woman.

At first a little disappointed, especially when romance reared its embarrassing head, she soon found she liked the idea of Mary Pickford growing up on the screen. In her green silk dress and the new short hairstyle Fay had encouraged her to try, she felt that in the last few weeks she'd done more than a little growing up herself.

She wondered in amusement whether she should write to Molly and warn her about the hair but a letter would take almost two weeks to reach home and she would be there just as soon. In the comfortable darkness of the gilded cinema she prayed that Molly would be able to see her, even if it meant she'd be shocked by what she saw.

Her trips to the Brimstead Clinic were mercifully brief. She didn't meet Mr Stoneleigh again but the nurse who dressed her hand daily assured her that it was coming along very well. Neither Corelli nor The Fist showed up but each time she went that phone number, Jamica 3500, rang ever more loudly in her ears. However, between the sightseeing and the preparations for the big move to Dennsville she was soon able to put it to the back of her mind.

The fussing over suitcases and trunks, the checking and rechecking for this item or that reminded Nora of the bustle on board ship on the night before they disembarked. She tried not to think that when the time for departure came *they* would all be going in one direction and she, in the opposite.

On the Sunday of that hectic week that had begun in the 'Villa Dolorosa' and ended with Mary Pickford's coming of age, they all went to the beach at Coney Island. Here was another feast for the eyes. The promenade, filled with strolling day-trippers, was constructed from timber and was called, sensibly enough, a boardwalk. It stretched 10,000 feet along the seafront. The sand for the beach, Phil explained, was pumped from the bottom of the Atlantic Ocean.

In the huge Steeplechase Amusement Park beyond the boardwalk they took whirling, dipping rides before Nora reluctantly squeezed herself into one of Fay's swimming costumes. As soon as she hit the water she was glad she'd overcome her shyness. Her scar tingled in the salt water but her fingers, pale below the surface, moved comfortably if slowly.

It had been the best day of her holiday so far and as they headed home on a packed train she felt the wonderful shiver of pleasure at having been washed clean of all the heat and irritation of recent days.

Denis wasn't too keen on the idea of calling into Ryan's shop when they reached Wash-Basin Street, but Phil insisted, adding mysteriously that there was nothing to worry about. They soon discovered what he meant.

'I can't get over it,' old Mrs Ryan said after they'd been chatting for a while. 'That money, the twenty-five dollars that was stolen awhile back. Well, we got it back. Someone posted it here yesterday. Can you imagine that? Never happened in all my days in this city.'

She was disappointed to hear Phil and Fay and the boys

were leaving New York but was happy to know that Phil would be working at something he really liked for the first time in his life.

'That's the main thing, isn't it,' she contended, 'If you're not happy at what you're doing, you're at nothing.'

As they got ready to leave the shop Denis came out from his hiding place behind Phil.

'We'll be calling whenever we come to New York,' he told the old woman. 'We won't forget you, Missus. You been real good to us.'

'Ah, young Dinny,' Mrs Ryan sighed, 'A pure little gentleman you have there, Mr Canavan. And Ritchie too, of course. An old head on young shoulders, what.'

Back on the street no one mentioned the money that had been returned. All that was in the past now and it was time to look forward. The boys taunted each other cheerfully as Phil flicked absentmindedly through the *New York Evening Post* he'd bought in Ryan's.

'Dinny the Gintelman,' Ritchie teased, copying the shopkeeper's Tipperary accent.

'An ould hid on young showlders,' Denis answered in the same flat tones.

They chased gleefully along Wash-Basin Street until they reached the apartment house. Nora joined them as they sat on the steps without a let-up in their caffling. Phil and Fay were walking very slowly now and both stared at the newspaper in astonishment.

Nora grew uneasy. Whatever it was they were reading it wasn't good news. Even the boys for all their high spirits eventually sensed that something was wrong. Phil folded away the newspaper, his face clouded over with some dark secret.

'This can't be happening,' Nora told herself, 'Nothing is supposed to go wrong now.'

Fay tossed the door keys towards the boys. Ritchie won the scramble to catch them but Denis wasn't really trying.

'What's up, Fay?' he asked.

'Nothing. Take up the groceries, OK?'

The two brown paper carrier bags might as well have been filled with rocks, so slow and laboured was their progress inside.

'Best sit down, Nora,' Fay advised when the boys had gone from sight.

'It's Corelli, isn't it?' Nora muttered, 'Something's happened to Corelli.'

She gripped the metal railing by the side of the steps with her quickly-healing hand. The pain was distant but it was still there to be felt.

'He's been shot,' Phil explained. 'Says here he's not expected to live. Seems that guy The Fist was hit too.'

'Was it Ruby?' she asked, knowing that if it was, all their plans were in ruins.

'Doesn't say,' Phil told her, 'Then again, it wouldn't, would it. Not in the newspaper. Even if it was true.'

'What's going to happen now?'

The question, Nora knew, was pointless. Nevertheless, it repeated itself in her mind like a chant. The kind of chant that helps you stop thinking, of imagining the worst. But it didn't last long enough to give her any comfort.

'Time will tell,' Phil said, shaking his head gravely.

All at once Nora was seized by a wretched feeling of guilt. Corelli, who had done so much for her, was dying and her only concern was for her brothers. She would have to go and see him.

'Does it say where he is?' she asked.

'Some private clinic,' Fay told her, 'It wouldn't be...?'

'The Brimstead,' Nora cried, 'Will you take me there, Phil?'

'I don't know if that's a good idea,' Fay objected.

'It's something I have to do. Please? Take me?'

They were soon on their way to the Brimstead. Phil, she guessed, was thinking about how his dream of freedom seemed to be slipping away. She tried to convince herself that thinking about such things now was foolish. Until they found whether Ruby had been involved in the shooting of Corelli they couldn't even begin to consider what the consequences would be.

'Whatever happens,' Phil said, 'you've done everything you could. Don't go blaming yourself if it doesn't work out, right?'

'Maybe I should have minded my own business.'

'It *was* your business. They're your kid brothers, after all,' he insisted, 'and I was going the wrong way about getting out of this mess.'

'You didn't have any other choice.'

All the while, a huge, fearsome resolve was growing in her. Perhaps, as Phil had said, there were no angels in this city but surely God was here somewhere and would listen. Don't let it be Ruby who shot Corelli or had him shot, she pleaded, and in return she would promise to take her place at the LaFonde Foundation. Besides, Corelli was dying. He had done everything in his power to make her happy and she must do the same for him.

Even as they left the city she was composing a letter to Ireland.

Dearest Molly and Peter,

I'm not very good at writing and maybe if I had better news it might come easier. There's only one way I can say this and that's straight out. I won't be coming home. It's such a long story it's hard to make sense of it, never mind write it down. But the long and the short of it is I had to make a promise to a dying man to save Denis and Ritchie from hell.

Words are useless, cruel and stupid things. Maybe that's why I love music so much. But the music to say what I feel would be too heartbreaking to write...

Soon her imaginary letter fell apart into a jumble of broken phrases as a vision of the kitchen in Stannix Lane intruded and refused to be dismissed. Peter and Molly sat at the big table with its heavy oilcloth cover. Molly's sightless eyes scanned the darkness as Peter read the hastily scribbled words. They both seemed immensely old as if the scene was set many years from now and they tried once again to understand why she had left them so long ago.

The Brimstead Private Clinic came into view, its bright walls concealing the suffering within just as Nora's brave face hid the unfair share of pain she'd endured in her short life. Phil paid the cab-driver and they entered the clinic. At the reception desk he asked a young man if Corelli had been brought here. The man looked at them frostily and shook his head. Nora walked past the desk and headed down the echoing corridor. Stretching out over the desk, the unhelpful receptionist yelled after her.

'Hey, lady! You can't go in there!'

She ignored him and went on. All week when she came here she'd seen no one at that desk. There could only be one reason why it was manned now. Phil ran to catch up with her as she turned the corner at the end of the corridor. When he found her she was standing by a doorway guarded by two police officers. By her side was The Fist looking bleary-eyed and bedraggled, his arm in a sling.

'But I have to see him,' Nora was shouting.

'It's awful bad, kid,' The Fist pleaded, 'You don't wanna see how...'

He punched the wall beside and the plaster splintered like ice.

'Hey,' one of the police officers warned, 'You can't control yourself, you're outa here.'

There was blood on The Fist's knuckles but he didn't seem to notice. The question on the tip of her tongue refused to be asked. Phil too was afraid to ask.

'I'm going in,' she said, steeling herself for the awful prospect ahead.

She made to step past The Fist but he held on to her. His grip was as firm but gentle as his words.

'He's already dead,' he whispered, 'He said to tell you, thanks for everything you done for him.'

Nora reeled back towards Phil. The slippered footsteps of patients and nurses in the corridor sliced through her head.

'Who shot him?' Phil blurted out no longer able to contain himself.

At once, the last pieces of this bloodstained jigsaw fell into place in Nora's mind.

'Lefty Feeney did it,' she uttered and they looked at her askance.

'How'd you come to know that?' The Fist asked.

'I'm right, aren't I?' she said and it all flashed before her eyes. 'He blamed you and Mr Corelli for what happened to Danny and now Ruby's got what he's always wanted — Vincent's life. And he's taken Lefty back into his gang and there's going to be a war between your gang and his. And Ruby's going to make Phil help him rob the bank and...'

She didn't realise that by now she was screaming at the top of her voice and beating her fists against the big man's chest.

'You got it all wrong, kid,' The Fist was saying, 'You got it all wrong.'

Phil pulled her away from The Fist and had to shake her because she was hitting him now.

'Nora,' he insisted, 'Listen. Listen to what he has to say. Take it easy now. It's gonna be alright.'

She sucked in a rasping breath and remembering the Countess at the Foundation she closed her eyes and forced herself to breathe steadily. When she opened her eyes she was dizzy but much calmer.

'Yeah, it was Lefty,' The Fist explained, 'but Ruby wasn't impressed. He lost his cool and...well, early this morning he had Lefty shot. He sent us a message, said it was a token of his good faith.'

Three people were dead and even if none of them was entirely innocent it still seemed horrific to Nora. The fact that she might have had some part to play in their deaths haunted her.

'This is all my fault,' she cried.

'Don't talk crazy. This kind of thing was goin' on long before you ever came to New York and it'll go on long after you leave,' The Fist told her. 'You made the Boss happier than I ever seen him since Oriana died. He knew this was coming. No one stays lucky forever.'

Nora was only half-convinced. Banishing the vision of Molly and Peter's hurt she spoke with a cold finality.

'I've been offered a place at the Foundation and I'm going to take it. I owe it to Mr Corelli.'

'You can't do that,' Phil exclaimed.

The Fist looked at her, his expression a mixture of gratitude and sorrow.

'I'm sorry, kid,' he sighed, 'but the money just ain't there no more. See, two days back, the income tax guys moved in on us. They've tied up every last dollar and it's gonna stay that way for years. They wouldn't even let us take him back to the house like he wanted. That's gone too. He ain't got a nickel to his name. I gotta pay for the clinic here outa my own pocket. After this I'm skint.'

It was hard to avoid the guilty sense of relief she felt at that moment. However, after long days of agonised doubt she came to accept that what had happened to Corelli had to happen some time.

As for Danny and his father, she realised that, if they hadn't tried to double-cross Ruby over this particular bank job, they would certainly have tried it at some point in the future. The result would surely have been the same.

These people lived dangerously and even when they began to change, as Corelli had, it was almost always too late. What happened to Danny was above all an awesome reminder of what might have been in store for Denis had she not intervened.

The best she could hope for Corelli was that some day his daughter, Maria, might stand at his graveside as Nora had once imagined. There, she might begin the slow, difficult journey to forgiveness. At the very least, if The Fist was to be believed, Nora had brightened his life for a short while. That was better than a promise she could only have kept with such a heavy heart that she might one day grow to hate his memory.

Her stay nearing its end another, more pleasant surprise rescued her from these sad thoughts. Phil announced that since they had no reason for staying in New York they would leave right away for Dennsville. This would give Nora a chance to see where her brothers' future lay and to see a little more of the vast American continent. When the time came, he would travel back with her to meet the triumphant hurlers at the SS *Bremen*. Apparently John and his team-mates had won all of their games in America, but the newspapers carried few details of their games and when they did there was too much happening for Phil or any of the rest of them to think of looking.

Nora was delighted with this new plan. Dennsville might be even further from Tipperary than New York but once she'd seen it she might more easily imagine their lives there. Besides, getting ready to leave would occupy the boys' minds and keep them from thinking about her departure.

None of them was sorry to descend those rickety stairs for the last time. When they piled into the taxi-cab and drove away from Wash-Basin Street no one looked back.

CHAPTER 22

Pennsylvania Station was the most incredible example she'd seen yet of this city's strange passion for buildings in the Roman style. She'd counted at least thirty broad pillars along its front before being swept on the tide of bodies through the grand entrance.

Inside, the great steel-ribbed, vaulted spaces were covered with acres of glass shaped into domes and arches. How Phil found his way around the crowded train concourse was a mystery to her. In fact, so assured did he look that more than once he was the one being asked for directions. Soon they were sitting in the Leigh Valley 'Chicagoan' and its thrumming engine calmed their racing hearts.

It was clear to Nora from all their faces that with the moment of departure so near, their feelings of anticipation were laced with some regret. She knew quite well that even if the place you are leaving holds many bad memories it is still painful to go and begin all over again elsewhere. She was sure they had good memories too as she'd had of Dublin and while these passed through their minds she remained silent, knowing it was better not to intrude.

However, as the 'Chicagoan' eased out into the sunlight and snaked its way beyond the city's edge, the boys perked up quickly. Phil and Fay, sitting side by side, locked arms as if to embolden each other for the passage to the rest of their lives.

All through the overnight train journey they sat up too full
of wonder and expectation to rest. The landscape Nora saw
before dark descended was very different to the one she had
grown familiar with on her train-trips to Dublin. Everything
was magnified and multiplied. Towns, cities, forests, plains,
sheer distances. The vast scale of the place spoke of release,
escape, and an overwhelming desire to explore every last
inch of it. Life, it seemed to declare, was full of possibilities
and the only limits were those you set on yourself. What
tremendous music should fill these distances. What sympho-
nies, underscored by the changing rhythms of the train travelling on and on and on and in the red glow of dawn arriving
at the prairies' edge, at Dennsville.

At the railroad station, Frank Thompson, Phil's friend,
greeted them. He had a lazy, cheerful kind of way about him
that seemed to mirror the relaxed atmosphere of the town
itself. They drove through a wide main street, that was busy
but somehow less frenetic than New York. People stopped
and talked to each other among the buildings that were
human in scale and wouldn't have looked out of place back
home in Tipperary.

Soon they'd left the car and were being shown around a
large two-storeyed timber-frame house. It had a small front
garden and a longer one at the back, at the end of which were
three tall apple trees. Ritchie bit delightedly on the yellow-red
fruit but his face screwed up as the sourness spilled over his
tongue. Denis tried another of the trees and whooped with
pleasure.

'They're beauties,' he cried and they all tasted the sweet
promise of the good earth.

Phil and Frank talked for a long time on the back porch of
the house, sitting comfortably in the easy chairs there. After
something of a struggle Fay managed to get the boys inside
to help Nora and herself to sort out the few bits and pieces

they'd brought with them.

The interior of the house was cool and fresh with the smell of polished wood. Each room was larger than the biggest one at Wash-Basin Street. Each one too was fully furnished and hung with bright, airy curtains. There were four bedrooms and the boys agreed without argument which one each would have as his own. Yet, when it came to sleeping that night they shared the one room.

'Just for tonight,' Ritchie said sheepishly, 'so's we can get used to the place.'

Out on the back porch, Nora sat with Phil and Fay for a long time that evening as the boys played in the garden. Warm and still, the sky seemed immense above them. Crickets gossiped in the grass and from further off came the faint stirrings of the town coming to rest.

'You like it?' Phil asked of Nora.

'It's perfect.'

'Frank says we can buy this place if we get a deposit together in six months,' he told Fay. 'He reckons we'll have no problem doing that.'

'I guess we found ourselves a home at last, Phil,' Fay declared and kissed him on the cheek.

Nora wasn't embarrassed. Fay had every right to be happy and to show it. This was as perfect a home as anyone could imagine and Nora was glad she'd had a chance to see it, if only for a few days. As they basked in the evening sun, it was her own home in Tipperary that Nora's mind returned to. The weeks before had been so hectic that she'd had little time to realise how much she truly missed it. Whenever the house in Stannix Lane had come into her thoughts it was simply as a place to escape from the pain and disappointment of Wash-Basin Street. Now she just wanted to be there with Molly and Peter because she felt she belonged there.

She thought about her return and instead of worrying

whether Molly's operation had been a success she resolved to accept whatever the outcome was, just as Molly would. If blindness was to be her aunt's fate, then she would do all she could to help.

Instead too of worrying about her eventual departure from Tipperary she realised that Molly and Peter wanted that bright future for Nora as much as she wanted it herself. And besides, she would always have that home to go to. It would always be there for her, she knew, no matter how far she travelled from it.

Phil stretched back in his chair, closed his eyes and began to speak in the words of some poet. Words that seemed to say everything that needed to be said.

'I strayed though the mist of the city
Like one distracted or mad.
"Oh, Life. Oh, Life," I kept saying,
And the very word seemed sad.

I passed through the gates of the city
And I heard the small birds sing,
I laid me down in the meadows
Afar from the bell-ringing...'

There would be sad moments in the next few days. Taking leave of Denis and Ritchie would not be easy in spite of all the banished doubts. Saying goodbye to Fay, with her easy-going charm and the tough spirit of survival beneath, would be more difficult than she could ever have imagined back in the dog days of New York. And Phil too, his good nature revived after the trials of the city.

And there would be another small, unexpected sadness that she could not have imagined as she sat listening to Phil on that bright evening.

'In the depth and bloom of the meadows
I lay on the earth's quiet breast.
The poplar fanned me with shadow
And the thrush it sang me to rest.'

At Hoboken Pier as she waited to board the SS *Bremen*,
John Moloney would have something to tell her. She'd be
surprised that it mattered to her but it would. When he'd say
he was staying in America she would laugh but it would be
true and she'd be truly sorry. She would blush at the tear in
his eye and his telling her that of all the things he'd miss, he'd
miss her most. And she'd blush too at the certain knowledge
that they'd be together again somehow.

But then she'd meet Hans on the ship and have so much
to tell him. She would play the grand piano, hesitantly at first,
and even dance in the gracious lounge, elegant in Fay's
dresses, unafraid to smile and be happy and lift, as she knew
she must, the soul-breaking weight of sadness in this world.

And the port of Cobh would swim into view, its houses
seeming to cling as if to a cliff face, proving you could make
a life in any circumstances no matter how impossible it might
sometimes seem. She would stretch her scarred hand along
the painted deck rail and feel that, yes, she could reach a full
octave with it and perhaps more. But it wouldn't matter if she
couldn't because she knew she would find a way to overcome
any handicap. Her thoughts would be filled with this evening
in Dennsville and Phil's voice softly rippling the silence with
the last stanza of a poem she would never forget.

'Blue, blue was the heaven above me
And the earth green at my feet;
"Oh, Life. Oh Life," I kept saying
And the very word seemed sweet.'

ALSO FROM WOLFHOUND PRESS

MELODY FOR NORA

One girl's story in the Civil War

Mark O'Sullivan

Nora is a survivor — and music is her lifeline.

The Civil War has just begun — the times are explosive and threatening. Nora's life is changed by her mother's tragic illness and a drunken father who cannot cope. She is sent to an aunt and uncle in Tipperary who may as well be strangers.

Here to her surprise is a cinema, and an eccentric piano-player, Alec, with a haunting melody. And here Nora finds herself forced to play an unexpected role in the unfolding intrigues and conflicts of her time.

Melody for Nora is a powerful novel of heartbreak in a troubled family, of living through civil war, and of a young girl's extraordinary resourcefulness.
ISBN 0-86327-425-0

DONNY GOES FOR GOAL!

Joe Buckley

Donny is struggling to keep his place on the senior soccer team, patch things up with Jacky and generally steer clear of trouble. But life for Donny could never be that simple! Follows the action-packed *Run, Donny Run!* and *Donny in London*.
ISBN 0-86327-415-3

JUDITH AND SPIDER

Mike Scott

In her well-to-do world, Judith sometimes wonders whether she'll ever see Spider O'Brien again. But why does Spider wish he'd never met her? Follows *Judith and the Traveller*, also by Mike Scott in the ACE Fiction Series.
ISBN 0-86327-347-5

BREAKING THE CIRCLE

Desmond Kelly

When Sorcha joins an environmental group, things start to move — fast! Marches, slogans and rousing meetings follow, but the others have some dangerous ideas. Sorcha has to decide how to act. At what price does the Circle want secrecy? And is her new friend Roger all that he seems?
ISBN 0-86327-348-2

MERLIN'S RETURN

Ron Langenus

The Second Time, night at Stonehenge. A young Merlin reappears after fourteen centuries...and he is getting younger! This time, Merlin is living backwards: the big question is 'why?' — and who is polluting the planet and where are King Arthur, Excalibur and the Knights?

But Merlin needs help to cope with this strange Twentieth Century and to solve the riddle that will lead to the powers of Camelot. He's joined by seven adventurous friends and Rex the terrier whose tail becomes crucial to their plans! Accompanied by the secret weapon made by Wizzo to Merlin's age-old design, the group take on Mordred and his S.I.A. (Sneaks in Action) and prepare to save the world....

But will King Arthur and his sword still have their powers after all these years and will Merlin find out why he's living backwards before he gets so small that he disappears???

'Full of excitement' *Irish Independent*
ISBN 0-86327-383-1

Available from your bookseller of from
Wolfhound Press
68 Mountjoy Square,
Dublin 1
Tel 01 874 0354. Fax 01 872 0207
Call or write for our catalogue